Finding Grace Again

BETH JANNERY

WCP

World Castle Publishing, LLC
Pensacola, Florida

Copyright © Beth Jannery 2014
Print ISBN: 9781629891866
eBook ISBN: 9781629891873
First Edition World Castle Publishing, LLC, December 15, 2014
http://www.worldcastlepublishing.com

Licensing Notes

Cover: Karen Fuller
Editor: Brieanna Robertson

Dedication

Thank you to all the special women in my life for showing me how to find grace again. Especially for Marti Jannery, my mom. And for my darling daughters, Skye and Tess. May you always instinctively know to turn to your Higher Power when you need strength. A heartfelt thank you to my incredibly kind and nurturing "old school" editor Hillel Black. Hillel edited the likes of Sidney Sheldon, as well as The New York Times bestselling MASH book, before it was a movie or popular TV series. His willingness to work with me is humbling. Thank you, Hillel, for helping me to have the courage to put words to paper and become a storyteller. I believed you when you said, "Beth, you are a storyteller. It is what you must do." This story would not exist without his tough love. Lastly, I have deep gratitude for my new editor Brieanna Robertson, who made this story so much better. Her patience and understanding—sometimes into the wee hours of the night—is a gift. While she didn't always agree with decisions I made in my craft, she showed a curiosity that demonstrated she cared about novel-writing as an art. Her words and suggestions were always to make this manuscript better while remaining respectful of what I wanted to do as a writer.

Chapter One

Regan Concord had a chance to live two lives. One
was the life she thought she was supposed to live. She
made it all look good on the outside. The second was one
she didn't know yet. This was her authentic life, the one
no one else owned, where she could be whatever the hell
she wanted. But this realness was buried down deep. Only
hitting a complete rock bottom could force Regan to start
digging for the life she was meant to live.

There are major life events that define people,
moments of clarity that mark time in a new way. For
Regan, her moments of there-is-no-going-back were
coming. She would wear them like tattoos—before and
after.

There would forever be before the affair and after the
affair. Then there was before the accident and after the
accident. Before the affair, Noah, Regan's handsome
husband, an Ivy-League-educated attorney, would kiss
her goodbye in the mornings. Before the accident, Regan
loved inhaling her 5-year-old daughter's hair, especially in
the morning in bed together after mixing with a night of
sleep. The deep scent of bed-head and Johnson's Baby

Shampoo comforted Regan; she was grateful not to have to jump out of bed at dawn to rush Grace off to childcare. They were lazy together, those two girls, sometimes watching morning TV in bed together, rereading "The Giving Tree" for the umpteenth time, or talking about the day to come. School days gave the girls a more organized routine and structure to the morning, but Noah got an earlier start to try to beat the traffic.

"Bye, sweets," Noah said. Mornings flowed together, the days blended, it was a peaceful existence.

"Bye, babe," she yawned, and rolled over, pulling Grace's warm body closer into hers. "Dinner at six o'clock. If you're going to be late again, call first." She grabbed his hand. He stood over Regan and Grace by the side of the bed. His fingers were cold.

Regan was well aware of Boston traffic. The big dig was complete, but everyday traffic jams at rush hour were commonplace, at least for Noah they were. She could never figure out how her husband always made a meeting with a CEO or a CFO on time, but was chronically late for the dinner table. She'd set the table for three, inevitably pushing dinner back to 6:30 p.m. or 7 o'clock, but Grace would get cranky and have to eat. Then the phone call would come—traffic was a bitch, or there was an accident, or a late meeting was called. She knew the drill. She gave up asking questions. It was never her battle to win. She should be grateful she could stay home with Grace and the bills were paid. She should be more compassionate and understanding and grateful. The evening routines got predictable, even to a kindergartener.

"Traffic again?" Grace asked.

"Yes, Daddy is in traffic."

Regan hugged Grace tighter.

"Daddy said to give you this." Regan gave Grace a big bear hug.

"Pinch and skeeze?" Grace asked.

"That's right, a pinch and a squeeze," Regan answered, smiling. Then she'd kiss the tip of her little nose and let out a "honk."

"Honky honk honk." Grace erupted into giggles.

Then bath time came, then stories, then a "night night, sleep tight tight," and then a chilled glass of Chardonnay after the lights were out.

Regan knew the life of an attorney's wife. She knew what she signed up for. The less she questioned it the better. Still, the loneliness sometimes got the best of her. She stopped waiting up for Noah. She stopped expecting anything different. His dinner plates sat alone under Saran Wrap and the dimmed kitchen chandelier. She did away with making family plans on weekends. She began going through the motions. And all this was before the affair, or at least before she had proof of his betrayal.

"Bye," he called to her from the hallway. "Don't wait up."

"Don't wait up?" A sick, knowing feeling welled up in her gut. She did what she could do to push down her fear. She suspected what was going on, but she couldn't say for sure. Perhaps she wasn't ready to know. Regan delighted in keeping up appearances. This made her feel safe, protected even. If it looked good on the outside then everything must be okay. It was all a farce, but it was the life she was willing to live, at least for now.

****

Regan Concord was in her therapist's office for the third time this week. She could tell a total stranger her pain. The therapist was paid to listen. Anyone closer, she pushed away.

"I knew his text was the final nail in the coffin," Regan told the therapist. "I knew he might really love her, but I wasn't ready for him to walk out the door. If anyone was going to decide to leave the marriage, it should have been me." Regan was angry. The text had read, *"U r right. I do luv her. Im leaving. Im sorry."*

This was Regan, always trying to control everything, even her husband's affair. Noah had told her in a text that he was in love with this other woman. Regan had seen the two of them together. If she hadn't, she may have been able to talk herself out of believing that there was actually another woman. All those nights Noah said he was working late. They were all lies.

He swore to her that he never saw this coming. He did admit to the affair, after he had been caught, but he insisted she meant nothing to him. In some small way, thinking the other woman meant nothing to Noah except physical sex was forgivable. Anyone could be tempted by sex; this rationale was weak, but it was all Regan had. *It's just sex*, she would tell herself. He didn't love this other woman; it was just once. Regan churned these justifications around and around. They gave her temporary comfort.

"It just happened," he'd lied.

"How does fucking another woman in our bed *just happen*?" Regan wanted to know.

The words Noah texted Regan were drawn in her memory like stains of blood. He planned to leave her for the other woman. Regan thought her worst nightmare had come true.

"It's like they are etched into my eyelids'" Regan told the therapist. "The only thing I see are these words." She grasped onto a drenched handful of tissues. "And then the sound of the metal, the screeching, the horns, the jolt." She crossed her arms. "I can't see or hear anything else. I went through a red light at forty miles per hour." The police said she never slowed down. It was as if there was no intersection, no red light, and no danger whatsoever.

"Then what happens?" The therapist was gentle about the way she asked, pushing Regan to continue, to purge herself of the details. She has recounted the story, factually, over and over to police officers, but this was the first time her tears don't stop falling. It was as if they would never stop and she would drown in them.

"The truck slams into the passenger side and I hear the crush, I feel the wave. It's so fast and it stops all at once. It's supersonic and it's paused." Regan added, "I remember everything and nothing." She was sobbing now, her eyes swollen and watery, her shirt wet from perspiration. She was shaking.

"It's important that you keep going," the therapist encouraged.

Regan continued, her voice cracking. She sounded almost-childlike. Her body was molding into a ball. Fetal position felt familiar to her. "I see Grace's hair. It's like a whip. It hits my cheek. She is being thrown from the backseat. I feel her skin and her arm, her delicate arm, as I reach for her with my hand. She slips out of my grasp." Regan talked slowly, very slowly. She didn't leave out any details. She was quiet for a few moments, then she opened her mouth. "She's gone," was all that came out. "Grace is gone."

Later, after the therapist handed Regan a glass of water, she asked her to describe the rest of the scene. Regan closed her eyes and did as she was told. She'd been coming to see this therapist for a while now and she knew it was important for her to heal.

"Well," Regan began, "Grace was alive one moment, singing along to the music, and gone the next."

"But what do you feel?" the therapist asked her.

"I feel profound sadness and utter grief." She thought back to the accident scene. "Then I vomit when I see her mangled torso. I throw myself on her body and blood and parts. I recognize nothing."

"Then what?" The therapist wouldn't stop.

"Jesus, isn't this enough?" Regan was getting angry. She said she felt like dying. She said she should have died that day, not Grace.

"What do you feel now?" the therapist interrupted, pushing for more.

"I don't know what I feel." Regan was unwilling to dig deeper.

"Tell me what you see."

"What do I see?" Regan was confused, disoriented.

"Yes, describe it. Describe what you see," the therapist instructed.

"My body is aching and I'm tangled and bruised. Glass is shattered. What do I feel? Like nothing is ever going to be the same. I feel like I want to die. Like I should die."

"Good," the therapist responded. "Keep going."

"What else? I guess I'm angry." Regan grew quiet. "I'm confused why I'm still here. Why did God take Grace and not me?" It was more of a statement than a question. "And the world feels cruel. Like someone is playing a horrible joke. Like I'm going to wake up at any minute. Nothing makes sense."

"What else, Regan? What else?"

"I can't find Grace. I'm looking everywhere and calling her name. I'm screaming for her and she won't answer me. Grace won't answer me." Regan went silent. Then, a low guttural sound came from deep within her. It was a purely animalistic sound.

"What else?" The therapist wouldn't stop. "Regan! You were texting while you were driving. What else?"

Regan dropped, she folded over. Her eyes were closed now. She was remembering and began to rock back and forth. She could barely breathe. She tried to describe the accident scene in more detail. She found Grace and crouched down over her daughter. She felt her blood and skin penetrate into her thin shirt. She tried to cover her dead daughter like a protective blanket.

Time passed. It could be minutes or hours. Regan looked around at her. She saw Grace's LL Bean flowery backpack a few feet away. She saw her fairy lunch bag and her kindergarten papers and folders blowing around in the street. Everything stopped. Regan was silent.

"What is it?" The therapist tried one more time, in a more compassionate and sympathetic tone. "What is it?"

"I smell her," Regan whispered. She remembered burying her face in the crook of Grace's neck, inhaling the scent of her hair. Then, getting louder and rocking faster, Regan exhaled, "I can't smell my daughter anymore."

BETH JANNERY

Chapter Two

They all came. Friends, acquaintances, work colleagues, and distant relatives from both Noah's side and from my side. *Will they ever leave?* This is all I could think about. They seemed to stay forever. Even people who were barely strangers lingered around after the coffee cups and dessert plates had been washed. Everyone offered to help. Experiencing the death of a child renders people helpless. Nothing prepares you for it.

There was a revolving door of people pouring in to offer condolences, flowers, fruit baskets, and casseroles. I watched them all come. I memorized the faces, the appropriate dark clothes, sensible heels, and lack of smiles. I counted the people who obviously didn't use a roll of masking tape before heading out the door; the dog owners were easy to spot. The other mothers were also recognizable. Red, glossy eyes and stained shoulders from burping babies or crusted food spots from kid's fingers. My black suit was properly dry cleaned, no longer showing evidence that I was a mother.

My mind went blank from time to time during the days spent mourning—the funeral and calling hours, the wake seemed to go on for an eternity, then it would all be over, abruptly over, something I had not expected. In the meantime, I had mini-blackouts. I'd see the parade of mourners come in, stand in line, get extra emotional over the sight of a little coffin. It was nearly impossible not to choke up, even if you didn't know Grace well. Just the image was enough to bring anyone to tears. During this time, I'd go in and out. I'd find myself calculating Grace's age.

I fixated on calculating how old she would be when she would be allowed to wear her first mascara or lip gloss, how old she'd be for her prom or for her graduation, or for her wedding. How old would I be? Of course, I knew these milestones would never come, but I kept calculating. I'd do the math and crunch the numbers in between cordial hugs and awkward exchanges of, "I'm so sorry, dear." Or, "I can't even imagine what you must be going through." The worst was, "I'll pray for you." No, even worse was, "God doesn't give us more than we can handle."

People say the stupidest things. If there was a proper way to grieve the death of a child, I'd follow the instructions to the last letter. But there is no manual about how to grieve. The grief comes in waves. It feels like it will never stop rolling in.

I didn't know how to act or what to say to anyone at Grace's funeral. It was during the sixth person of the hour who came up to me at her funeral, who said, "God must have needed Grace to do some work in heaven," when I really shut down. I wanted to scream, "No, I need Grace right here, next to me, on fucking Earth." Instead, I went into a mini-walking-coma, as I like to call it, where I found comfort in playing the numbers tape over and over in my head. Grace was five when she died. I always thought of us as connected. I was thirty when she was born, I was thirty-two when she turned two, thirty-five when she turned five, and thirty-five when she died. She would always be five to me.

I wondered if a mother was always a mother, even if their daughter was no longer there. Or, if when a child died, the mother got stripped of that title. That's what I wondered.

Certainly, a mother who texted while driving, a mother who drove through a red light, a mother who killed her five-year-old daughter in a car accident, deserved to be stripped of the honorable title of Mother. In and out of thought I went, all through the days, in and out, playing over in my head what I knew everyone was thinking but would not dare to say—that I killed my daughter. I was a monster.

They all came, one after the other, to say goodbye to Grace and to silently thank God that their children were home safe and sound. Then they came to look the monster in the eye, to give condolences but quietly pity the mother who killed her only daughter.

The movie *The Big Chill* ruined any funeral—I couldn't go to one without thinking of Kevin Costner lying in the casket, his friends coming to mourn the passing of him. Playing the corpse in the movie was one of Costner's early roles. I prided myself on knowing random trivia. Noah used to quip that I knew a little bit about everything, but not a lot about any one thing. This was opposite of his vast knowledge of the law. As an attorney, it was in his blood to know everything. He was an expert on several aspects of the law. I used to defend myself to his critique, reminding him that I was the best damn mother in town. I was forever reminding the father of my daughter that I was the master engineer of our household.

"Hey, I may not have been published in the Law Review, but I've got *Goodnight Moon* and *Rainbow Fish* memorized." This would usually shut him up for a little while. Noah would never come right out and criticize me for not using my degree, but he was of the mindset that a nanny could do my job. He missed the old Regan, the one who had rose-colored glasses on who was ready to take on the world. He expected me to be a career woman, and when I found contentment staying at home, I seemed to go down a couple of notches in his eyes. But I was okay with that, because I was the best mom in town. Now I couldn't even claim that title. My standing in the community fell; I was alone at ground zero.

Now, at every funeral, I heard the opening song from *The Big Chill*. It was always one of my favorite Rolling Stones songs. The lyrics played in my head over and over and over. I thought everyone else heard them too. I wish I could shut out the sound of noses being blown, shoes scuffing, and shushed whispers in the corner. The background noise turned down and I put on my invisible iPod and played the Stones song to serve as a reminder that I don't always get what I want, but I get what I need. More people came. Strangers to me. I kept counting.

When I was forty, Grace would be ten. When I was forty-five, she should turn fifteen. When I was fifty, Grace would be twenty. I saw her through preschool and into kindergarten, but I'd never see her through elementary school, or middle school, or her period. No bra shopping. No, *"Are You There God? It's Me, Margaret,"* talks. No college. No wedding. No children. No grandchildren. I began to worry how I would survive Mother's Day.

I heard what everyone was saying.

"Thank God that's not my daughter."

"I don't know what I'd do if I lost a child."

"She must feel terrible."

"How do you go on from here?"

"She'll never forgive herself."

"Accidents happen. But this was no accident, she was texting."

"It could have happened to anyone of us. But I'd never forgive myself."

"Why couldn't she wait to text?"

"Is it true about Noah having an affair?"

"How could he bring the other woman to her funeral?"

"They are getting divorced."

"She should have been paying attention while she was driving."

"It isn't her fault. She just found out he was cheating."

"It's her fault. She should have protected her child."

No one would say it, but they all thought it, I was sure of it—I killed her. I killed Grace. I wanted the voices to stop. I wanted everyone to go away. I wanted to turn to Noah for support. I needed my husband.

The police didn't even give me a reckless driving charge. It was pointed out to me, time and again, that no punishment would be worse than the life sentence I have been handed—my daughter was dead. They felt sorry for me. My punishment was life.

Noah didn't push to file any reckless driving charges. Instead, he asked for his freedom, or rather, he told me he was leaving, and I didn't fight it. He said a lot of things that had been on his mind—"There is no excuse for texting while driving, but I've done it too. I can't forgive; Grace is dead because of you. But I understand you were angry. I understand you were in shock that I was leaving. I'm sorry I told you that way, but I knew you'd talk me out of it if I told you in person. Our marriage was over a long time ago. Once Grace came along, I felt like I lost you completely. All I wanted was a little of your attention." Noah went on and on trying to explain himself, trying to make some sense out of what transpired. He took no responsibility and continued to blame me. I did not defend myself.

Regan nodded and listened. Her body language shut him out; she closed herself off from everyone. But deep down, she knew he was right. Then, right there at the funeral, she saw Noah's future. She saw him marrying the other woman, the woman she fondly referred to as "the bitch." Regan saw them marrying and the younger woman getting pregnant right away, probably the perfect nuclear family, a boy and then a girl, she assumed. They would give her Grace's name for a middle name. Noah would move on and begin again and create a little bubble of perfection.

The funeral was over. The events were done. We were wrapping up loose ends.

I was handed a container. Noah moved closer next to me. He held me up. It was a small gesture of kindness. I overlooked the fact that he brought "the bitch" with him. I was too numb to be angry. The bitch kept quiet and offered what she hoped would be a soothing smile. I found no comfort in it, but I recognized her effort in trying. I felt sorry for her; she never knew Grace.

The container, I knew, was the urn. I was holding a small, delicate urn that protected the burnt ashes of my daughter's little body. My hands trembled. I shook. I could not see for pools welling in my eyes. Nothing remained but ash and dust. I thought about what to do next. My mouth was dry. "I need some water."

"Here." Noah handed Regan a disposable plastic cup. She took a sip and her throat opened slightly. "Thank you," she responded.

"Oh, Regan," Noah whispered. He leaned into her neck. She let him, listened. "I'm so sorry... I never imagined it would come to this." She stopped him. She couldn't hear anymore. She nodded, letting him know that his words were not spoken in vain. She nodded. It was all she could do. "I never meant to hurt you...."

Regan walked away, Noah's words trailing off. She was someplace else now. Escaping. Running. She was in the woods with Grace, the leaves crackling underfoot. Regan kept walking.

When I was strong enough, I would scatter her body where we went acorn hunting. Or by the small brook where we spied on birds. Or in the waves where we jumped together holding hands last summer. Or in the grass where we counted our somersaults. Or in the field where we made dandelion headbands. Or into the wind.

Now, it was time to go home. I needed to make a plan. Perhaps put the house on the market and pack up. People told me I should start over. I thought starting over was a fancy way of saying running away.

Chapter Three

Friends and family had all left now. People went on with their lives. The hugs and condolences were gone. The revolving door no longer spun. I was sitting still for the first time in months. The last box was packed. I was about to tape it up.

I kept two boxes full of memories of Grace. Some were crafts that she made, and photos, but most were books. So many memories were created by sitting and reading together. Grace used to climb onto my lap.

"Read away," she'd say. Then at the end of the story, she'd wrap it up with a boisterous, "The End." She was still getting the grasp of how to pronounce the perfect T sound. Instead, something adorable like, "Dee End" would come out of her plump little rosy lips.

I stuffed a weathered Velveteen Rabbit into the last box. Beneath the plush toy was a well-read copy of the book of the same name. I scooped it up and pressed the pages into my chest. I knew exactly where to turn and I began reading.

I read aloud; I read as if Grace was sitting on my lap.

"*What is REAL?*" *the Velveteen Rabbit asked the Skin Horse one day. "Does it mean having things that buzz inside you and a stick-out handle?"*

"*Real isn't how you are made,*" *said the Skin Horse. "It's a thing that happens to you. When a child loves you for a long, long time, not just to play with, but REALLY loves you, then you become Real.*"

"*Does it hurt?*" *asked the Velveteen Rabbit.*

"*Sometimes,*" *said the Skin Horse, for he was always truthful. "When you are Real you don't mind being hurt.*"

"*It doesn't happen all at once,*" *said the Skin Horse. "You become. It takes a long time. That's why it doesn't happen often to people who break easily, or have sharp edges, or who have to be carefully kept. Generally, by the time you are Real, most of your hair has been loved off, and your eyes drop out and you get loose in your joints and very shabby. But these things don't matter at all, because once you are Real you can't be ugly, except to people who don't understand. But once you are Real you can't become unreal again. It lasts for always.*"

I hurt. Then, something powerful began to unfold. I was suddenly consumed with the knowledge that I had known real love. I had felt something real. My entire life was not a sham. Grace was real. My love for her was real. My love for her is real.

Still, I hurt. I hurt so much I could no longer see the pages.

Chapter Four

The "For Sale" sign was replaced quickly by a "Sold" sign. Almost all the boxes were out. Her hands hated the feel of thick cardboard. Scratched up, chapped on the inside. Her fingers drank in the lotion. Regan made several trips to the kitchen sink where she'd press on the lotion dispenser and briefly feel satisfied. Otherwise, everything felt dry and cracked.

On the outside, she was barely holding it together. Her hair was up in a high ponytail and her last shower was at least a day or two ago. On the outside, she was cracking. On her insides, everything was already in pieces. She felt shattered.

Leaning over the kitchen sink, Regan splashed some cold water on her face. Her eyes burned. They were so dry. She applied eye drops several times a day, but her lids felt like the Sahara. Out the window, she could see a light dusting of snow; enough had stuck to make the holidays white. She used the last of the paper towels, her mind running through the past few months.

In the late summer, she took Grace on her first back-to-school adventure. They went shopping together. It was to be the first of many back-to-school shopping trips for supplies and clothes and shoes. They shopped for new clothes. Grace already had her own look. She had a passion for crazy-looking tights, she called them, or anything resembling a rainbow. She was drawn to anything striped or multi-colored or polka dotted and loved the easy, pullover dresses. Land's End seemed to have the sturdiest cotton, and the array of colors to choose from could withstand the kaleidoscope of paints and spills that would surely end up on her dresses. Regan never worried about play clothes vs. school clothes. She let Grace run and climb and paint in anything she had on.

They were planning after school activities and bought new school shoes. She loved red shoes. Regan found red wooden clogs from Hannah Anderson. While not very practical, they were adorable. She worried she might break her neck. Regan had small moments like that—she'd briefly forget that Grace was gone, but reality would come back soon enough. Regan knew this would fade overtime and soon enough, she'd begin to forget the details of her face and have to reach for photos for reminders.

Regan began looking around the house, searching for any remaining items she neglected to box up. She saw the hooks in the mudroom. Little Grace had grown inches over the summer; Regan was planning to raise the hooks. She sat down by the mudroom door, feeling weak. Never again would she have to stop in the mudroom to tie Grace's shoes. Regan bent her body in half, folding onto her knees, spreading her hands onto the floor, trying to grip the wood. There was nothing to grip, nothing to hold onto. She'd splinter her finger tips if the floor had been anything but perfect. Not even a thin film of grit transferred to her fingertips.

The ache grew. She emptied a waling sound. There was no one to soothe her. She quickly pulled herself together, as she often did, took one last photo with her cell of her empty house. It was only ever a home when Grace's footsteps echoed up and down the back hallway.

"Pumpkin, quietly please. You are not being raised by elephants," she'd shout to Grace in a loving, motherly voice, instructing her to use her inside voice. Grace was always so loud and coming out with the funniest expressions. Regan was certain the clomping of her footsteps could be heard all the way across the neighborhood cul-de-sac.

"Oh my God," Noah would say, "she's trouble." Then he'd laugh and they'd smile about Grace. With Grace, they knew they had done something right.

Sometimes, Noah would even say, "Hey, babe, at least we got that right." This was their way of acknowledging that not much else in their marriage seemed right, but both backed off the topic. It brought them together, for a brief moment, to be bonded in raising Grace and in experiencing her humor as she did something else cute or wild or silly or loud.

The conversation about their marital problems would be avoided and saved, perhaps, for another day. Neither Regan nor Noah seemed prepared to address the issues. Until something was said aloud, until it was spoken to another person, it didn't have to exist. It could stay in the dark, or under the bed, where the monsters hid.

She stood up from the mudroom floor and began locking windows and shutting off lights. She made her way slowly around the house, inhaling deeply as she walked room to room. Her plan was about to fall into place. The house went on the market right after the services, and it sold fairly quickly. Regan was grateful she lived in a nice Boston suburb. She didn't worry about having to drag out house showings because, fortunately, the market was in her favor. The house was snatched up by a couple with two school-aged sons. Regan didn't know them personally, but she assumed they had heard about her tragedy since they kept out of her business, didn't ask too many questions, which Regan appreciated.

In the weeks after Grace's death, people made suggestions. Mostly people said, "Give it some time." Regan didn't think she was rushing into anything. She knew what she was doing. She couldn't get out of there fast enough. She saw no point in being still; there could be no happiness until she was out of the house where her husband cheated, where her daughter's footsteps were no longer heard. She wanted to get on the road and drive away, open all the windows to the cold, winter air and never look back.

She'd have to sign divorce papers, of course, and finish the house sale with Noah, but she was fine with all of that. In fact, she opted out of spousal support and instead, agreed to all of the profits from the sale of the house. Noah gave it to her almost without asking, surely out of guilt for having the affair in the first place. He'd give Regan the money from the house, close the door on the past, and begin a new life with the younger woman.

This was fine with Regan, she was ready to be free to fly away. She wasn't about to fight for a man who didn't want her. People asked her what her plan was. It seemed everyone wanted to know where she was going and if she'd be back. The idea of going somewhere new, where no one knew her, sent a chill through her spine. She could be anyone she wanted to be. No one would know she had killed her daughter. She already looked forward to the freedom that came with looking strangers in the eyes and not seeing a speck of pity. She could hardly wait to blend in, and to disappear.

BETH JANNERY

Chapter Five

There was a one-year position, funded by a grant from the state that she stumbled upon while researching employment opportunities. It had been almost six years since Regan used her degree in social work. She'd always loved the Berkshires, so it is an easy decision to make. She was somewhat over-qualified for the position of managing a runaway shelter for teens. She learned that she was the only candidate with a master's degree. The whole decision to move happened quickly, all within one day. She went out for the interview, got the offer as Director of The Sojourn House for Girls, and found an old farmhouse to rent thanks to her deft research skills and impeccable timing on Craigslist.

Regan spent little time thinking about what to do next. She and Noah decided to put the house on the market, he moved out within a matter of days after Grace's death, and Regan made the decision to move to the other end of Massachusetts, a quaint area of New England referred to as "The Berkshires." It was charming place, somewhat sleepy, not too far away from civilization, but remote enough where she could slip in and go unnoticed. At least, this was her thinking. She mulled over other ideas as well.

Not knowing how to begin or where to look, she turned to stories she had heard of other divorced women who were starting over. She didn't have great role models: Alice from the 1970's TV sitcom *Mel's Diner* came to mind, but she didn't have a son in tow, and she certainly wasn't going to work at a truck stop diner serving eggs to strangers, though there was something appealing about going where no one knew her name because she could be whoever she decided to be. The other divorcee' reference that popped to mind was the single mom star of *One Day at a Time*, but she didn't have two teenage daughters played by Valerie Bertinelli or Mackenzie Phillips to play off of. There weren't many divorced women she held up as role models.

There was, of course, the lure of the divorcee' cliché. She considered her options after reading *Eat, Pray, Love* as well as *Under the Tuscan Sun*. But Regan figured those adventures were only for bestsellers and neither of the main characters—played by either Julia Roberts or Diane Lane—had a dead child in the mix.

Someone once said Regan's looks somewhat resembled Diane Lane, so that was an appealing option, but she couldn't see her life in Italy working out as grand as Lane's character had. In the book, she'd buy an Italian villa to restore and remodel, plant a vineyard, and fall in love with handsome, buff Italian men. No, this wouldn't work out for Regan. She knew her expectations would never be met. Besides, she had heard somewhere that Italian men had mistresses and she knew she could not handle another.

Regan opted for the less glamorous search for self — a year in the Berkshires to figure things out, stay under the radar, and work at a medium pace. She had no intention of staying, no desire to get to know anyone, and certainly no thoughts of actually living there after the year. Her plan seemed simple enough; she'd go to the Berkshires for one year and figure out what to do with the rest of her life.

Doing the final walk-through of her house, she felt completely alone. There were no more funeral services, no more casserole dishes to return, and no more real estate agents or attorneys to occupy her thoughts. The boxes were out of the house. Her bags were packed for the inn. She was expected to arrive in the Berkshires in a few hours. The thought of the Berkshires gave her a tiny amount of comfort. She knew there would be breathing space.

She finished turning off the lights and checking the windows. She stopped in the master bedroom, which was completely empty. She stared at the nail holes along the far wall. She counted them, remembering when Noah hung them. "Don't just eyeball them," Regan ordered. "Where's your level? Make sure they are even."

"Jesus, everything has to look perfect with you," Noah responded. She couldn't let anything go, he thought. This went for the hem on his pants, the polish on her shoes, and even the way she'd get ready for bed. Everything was orchestrated and she was the conductor, the director, and the producer. She would lay out clothes for the next day, neatly organize the pillows onto a corner chair in the bedroom, and dot her forehead, eyes, and neck with night cream before climbing in next to him.

Everything was always just so. There was even a right way to have sex. Even after sex, she would hop up and reach for a towel. Long gone were the days of carefree lovemaking and falling asleep with legs and arms in a knot. He missed falling asleep inside her.

Regan could be so cold. She stopped reaching for him at night. He knew the schedule, and any attempt at a variation of this was met in a scolding of sorts. He'd hear a deliberate sigh, and felt as if he was asking her to do him a favor. The rare event of actually getting a blow job was cause for celebration.

Once in a while, she'd go down on him, usually after an extra glass of wine and if he promised to get up with Grace in the morning and let his wife sleep in an extra hour. Noah would question, *When do I get to sleep in?* But he didn't dare say this aloud.

Noah was lonely. If Regan were to ask him, he'd say everything was fine. It wasn't until the idea of an affair was planted that he even realized how attention starved he was. He grew tired of Regan's rebuffs.

Regan never let anyone in, except for Grace. She was consumed with motherhood and keeping up appearances. The silent resentment in Noah began to build. One night, Noah tried to connect, coming home early to make dinner and add a little romance to the evening.

Regan couldn't roll with it. She was pissed dinner plans were changed, because she already had the meal organized. She had precut the vegetables, already chopped the salad fixings, and the chicken was marinating for six hours. She complained about being tired of running around with Grace all day. Truth was, Regan was looking forward to catching up with a few mindless shows from Bravo! she had DVR'd earlier in the week. She assumed Noah would be home after 9 p.m., as usual, and she'd have two hours to herself if she could get Grace down by 7 p.m.

"Watch your shows tomorrow," Noah suggested. "Let's open a bottle of wine." While Regan did as he asked, he could feel the resentment swell in her.

"You decide to come home early one night and expect me to drop everything and give you my undivided attention." Regan began the argument of the evening.

He avoided the confrontation as best he could. Noah didn't let up on his plans for romance. After dinner and wine, he cleared the dishes and Regan went to shower. She relished this time alone; the hot water did something to soothe her. There was no little one knocking on the door to come in, no one tugging on her leg to be picked up. Just as she was unwinding under the shower spray, she felt Noah's presence. He was coming into the shower with her, and she could see he was already getting hard.

"Great," she quipped. "The more the merrier."

What the fuck is your problem? Noah wanted to know, but didn't dare ask. Instead, he began to take her, gently pushing her against the shower tiles. She resisted.

"Can't we just have a night where we all we do is cuddle?"

Noah persisted, stroking her shoulders. Moving her wet hair away from her neck, he began to kiss behind her ear. Her body tensed. He felt her annoyance.

"Fine, hop on, the playground is open. I've had Grace climbing on me all day. Why don't you climb on too?" She thought that would be enough to deter him. She clearly wasn't in the mood for sex, and the thought of foreplay, well, she was simply too tired. Noah went ahead anyway. He bent her body over slightly and entered her from behind. She felt him stiffen; he became hard and unstoppable.

Are you fucking kidding me? she thought. He went ahead and did his business, climbing on her and cuming in a matter of a minute or two. As he grunted and thrusted deeper into her, she felt used and unappreciated. *This is all he thinks I'm good for,* she thought. Regan couldn't believe he was doing this.

She recalled how many times she had sex with her husband when she didn't want to. They were performing the most intimate act a husband and wife could share, yet she felt more disconnected than ever. He was clueless.

He finished, Regan cleaned herself up in the shower, and they got dressed for bed.

"Ah, I needed that," was all he could say.

Chapter Six

The thought of having an affair came to him at work, of all places. He discovered that most people who cheated did so with someone they worked with. It was true. He heard this tidbit one morning on one of those annoying morning talk shows. Regan often had a news show on in the background when he was getting dressed for work.

He even Googled the statistic and found the results staggering. The stats, while alarming, validated his behavior. During his research, he also learned that something like 80 percent of the men who cheated, did so while their wives were pregnant. Now, he'd never done that. He had been one of the good guys, even refraining from sex for two months because his wife had complained of discomfort during the last trimester. The stat showed him that he wasn't the only one messing around with a work colleague. It was more common than he ever imagined. If it was easy and right in front of you, and she gave you attention while you went home to a wife who pushed you away, well, who wouldn't cheat?

Self-justification? Perhaps, but the decision was made the first moment the woman at work made him stiffen. He hadn't felt this desired for years. To call the woman at work a colleague was being generous. Noah knew better than to screw another partner in the firm. He picked a low level marketing girl. She looked up to him, asked him questions about his big cases, and made him feel important. Noah recognized that he was the ultimate cliché. To add to the stereotype, she was younger and blonde.

He'd stay late at work for his office rendezvous and sometimes, he'd plan an outing and book a discreet hotel room. He started to take risks being seen in public, but he always invented some cover story, just in case. He was sure he could talk his way out of getting caught. She was a woman at work he was mentoring, or if push came to shove, she looked so young she could pass for Grace's nanny.

Noah had always done what Regan had asked, he even wore complimentary colors to events because she liked to match as a couple. He did what he had to do in order to keep up appearances. There was a certain expectation about being a partner in a top-Boston firm.

But around this new woman, he began to get too relaxed, sloppy even. Regan sometimes planned a getaway weekend with Grace, which made it easier to see his mistress. If he was working long hours, she would sometimes take Grace to visit her Godmother and her children. He was thankful for the break and he began planning some stolen time with the marketing girl.

Regan began to put a plan in place to surprise Noah. She started plotting away, working out the childcare details behind the scenes. She knew Noah wouldn't suspect a thing and the idea of arranging for a romantic night – kid-free – excited her. She knew Noah would appreciate it; it was not something he'd expect from her. She was well aware that she asked a lot of him and he asked so little of her. This was an attempt to show him that she did, in fact, appreciate him. Regan took delight in planning the surprise. Not only did it give her a sense of control, but the anticipation of some much-needed time under the sheets with her husband began to build. Having time without a baby, toddler, or kindergartener underfoot was all too rare.

Grace didn't need to be picked up until Sunday. Everyone left the house early Friday morning; the schools were off thanks to a teacher/staff development training day. Regan headed over to Grace's Godmother's house. It was a nice friendship. Camille lived north of Boston and had twins the same age, and it made for a convenient sleepover about every six months or so. The five-year-olds played so well together, and Grace's Godmother said it would actually help her get some things done since Grace was a built-in playmate. This would be perfect for a kid-free weekend. Regan vowed to return the favor.

Regan took care of the logistics and confided in Cam about sensing some distance in her marriage. The women commiserated about how marriage changed after babies. Regan's plan was in place. She'd be there, when he arrived home from work, freshly showered, with a new lavender massage oil. He'd be stunned. This would go a long way. When he got home from work, it might take him a little while to unwind from work-mode, but once she started rubbing his shoulders and back with the oil, she knew they'd be back to the way it was in no time.

She tried to reach Noah at work, but hung up when she got his voicemail. She was feeling a little naughty and wanted to tease him by talking dirty to build the anticipation for this evening. But all she got back was a text that read: *"in mtg ttyl."* She'd call back in a few minutes and leave a sexy voicemail if she didn't reach him. So far, most of the day was on schedule. She made it back to town by late afternoon, missing out on the crazy Boston traffic. This made her smile in relief. She liked it when life went as planned.

When Regan pulled into their driveway, she saw his black Range Rover in the semi-circle. She saw a smaller sporty car too, a cute, shiny, white BMW. A sick, confusing, sinking feeling took over her gut. What was going on? Why was Noah home during work hours? Was something wrong? A series of questions ran through her brain. He had just texted her saying he was in a meeting. What the hell?

She was instinctively quiet with the car door, but raced into the house, leaving her bags in the vehicle. Keys clutched in one hand, she opened the door with the other. It was unlocked. She knew he wasn't expecting her. She knew he had been thoughtless not to lock the door.

Her mind was working overtime. She was creating all these logical scenarios to explain why he was home in the middle of the day. None of the scenarios made sense.

They say a woman always knows. Down deep, she knew. She felt it. Looking back, she knew about the bitch before she saw her car. And she knew what was going on behind the bedroom door. Women always knew.

He said it was just sex.

In this moment, she crumbled. The cut of betrayal went so deep. She heard Noah and the bitch before she opened the door. She heard moans of, "Yeah, fuck me. Mmmm, I like that" before she saw his backside and a woman's shapely legs up in the air, spread eagle, toes pointed. Hot pink toe nails. She'd never forget.

He said he didn't love her.

Regan stood there, stunned, silently watching her husband screwing another woman, a younger woman, a squeaky and annoying woman. Regan couldn't move. She tried to look away. And then she saw it, her daughter's American Girl doll on the floor. She fixated on the doll.

She suddenly had no room for forgiveness, but also had no capacity to feel.

She went numb.

What kind of man fucked another woman in his own house, his own bed, where his daughter was made, where her doll lay on the floor? He had to step over the doll to get into bed. He didn't even see it.

That was the thing, he never noticed anything. He had stopped noticing Regan years ago. He resented her time spent with Grace. He wanted all her attention. He needed her. He had a void, left from his own mother. A void no woman would ever fill.

Regan knew the marriage had ended long before the affair. It ended when she stopped playing the role of nurturer, when she stopped catering to his every need. She stopped taking care of him.

For a while, she let the anger consume her. She had the bitch's look of surprise etched in her memory. Regan had no concept of time. She could have been standing in the bedroom doorway watching for a few minutes or a few hours, she had no idea.

"Oh my God, shit, your wife." The strange woman began scrambling around reaching for her clothes, as if covering up would bring a shred of decency to the situation.

"This isn't what it looks like. " Noah jumped up.

"Get my clothes," the woman demanded.

"This never happened before," Noah began, defending his actions. He looked like a deer caught in headlights. Frozen.

"This is the first time," Noah clamored. The bitch's face gave it all away. She looked pissed that the man she was screwing would lie about the affair. It was obvious to Regan this wasn't the first time.

Then awkward silence.

And then the truth.

"We love each other." The bitch's voice sounded like a sorority girl.

"Oh, you love each other? " Regan started laughing.

"Shit, Regan. You're supposed to be away. What are you doing home?" Noah was famous for shifting the blame onto her. This was one time she would not stand to be thrown under the bus. She'd done nothing wrong this time, other than walking in on her husband having sex in her marital bed.

"Where's Grace?" Noah inquired while hurrying to get dressed. He seemed puzzled as to why Regan was home without their daughter, and then in an instant, he connected the dots. "You were going to surprise me?"

"Yep, some surprise," Regan responded glibly.

"We can explain," the high-pitched voice said, looking at Regan with pity.

Lips moving.

More excuses.

"Don't bother, you mother fuckers. I fucking hate you." Regan whipped around, slamming the door behind her. "It's over. We're over. You fucking dick," Regan yelled from behind the door.

And.

Then.

She.

Stopped.

She wrapped into a silent cocoon. A blanket of stillness.

She didn't yell again. Didn't speak. All she saw was commotion. Everything moved around her.

She knew it was finally over.

As much as it hurt to be let go, Regan knew that she'd done the letting go a long time ago. She got married when she was unsure. She was too demanding at times. Or not enough at others. Her expectations were too high. Or she had none at all. There was no middle. She needed someone to take care of her, too.

Then this strange thought entered her mind. Noah was just an element of her life. He was not her entire life. She had Grace. Grace was her life...

Regan glanced at the time. She needed to get on the road if she was going to check into the inn on time. She took a final look at the bedroom and gently closed the door.

She walked downstairs to the kitchen and remembered all the sounds. She saw Grace in her highchair eating spaghetti for the first time. She watched Grace's face turn orange from mashed carrots and sweet potatoes. Regan remembered the countless cups of spilled milk she wiped from the floor, and the peas she pulled loose from Grace's nostrils. Regan began to laugh uncontrollably and then suddenly, she stopped, abruptly, wiping fresh tears.

She thought about how many times she had wrapped Noah's dinner in plastic wrap only to set it on the counter for when he got home late from work. She heard the beeping of the microwave and then the constant chiming of his smart phone indicating texting well after work hours. She listened for the cold clicking of his wingtips on the kitchen floor, the opening of the utensil drawer, and then the fast running of water and the shutting of the dishwasher. His dinner for one. She shut her eyes.

The wife apron never really fit her.

She exited the mudroom, got in her car, and backed out of the driveway for the last time. She headed to the Massachusetts Turnpike and drove west.

Chapter Seven

Regan stopped on the Mass Pike at a truck stop on her way from Boston to the Berkshires. To add to the vibe, she had in an old James Taylor CD and she was signing along with JT. Her mind began to calm as James lulled her into a meditative state as he described the cold December air with the turnpike covered with snowflakes all the way from Boston to Stockbridge. It felt like he was singing directly into her as she disappeared into her dreamlike trance. Hard miles behind her and so many more to go...

Regan fell in love with truck stops as a kid. She remembered a family trip. It was the middle of the night and their tire blew. The whole family was awake and together and she saw this other world that intrigued her. At night, when little girls turned off lights and went to bed, the rest of the world didn't sleep.

This discovery made her feel less alone. Whenever she couldn't sleep as a child, she'd think about the commotion going on at the rest stops all over America's highways. There was this underbelly of society that fascinated her. She imagined their lives. There were lovers on the road and strangers meeting at night. She had discovered a place where no one ever slept. Someone was always awake. She felt less alone.

Regan had been on the road for over an hour. She pulled into the truck stop and made her way toward the diner with a bundle under her arm.

"Just one?" the overweight hostess asked.

"Yes, table for one," Regan replied evenly. She slid into the greasy booth and placed a stack of unopened cards to the side. She accepted the menu from the hostess and gave an obligatory half-smile.

"We serve breakfast all day," the hostess said as she walked away.

She settled in and began reading the condolence letters about Grace. Regan never looked up when the waitress came over to ask if she wanted coffee.

In the cards, no one mentioned the divorce. A few Christmas cards were mixed in. She sorted through the correspondence. People were careful choosing their words. Often, there was much said in the unsaid.

Finally, Regan took a sip of her coffee. "Strong coffee," she said in an attempt to make small talk to the waitress, who was ready for her order.

"What'll you have?" The server shifted leg to leg while she wrote down the short order. "How do you want your eggs?" Regan always ordered sunny side up. If one cracked, she would send the pair back.

She began to open the last card. This was something she must do before moving on to the inn—before starting over.

The inn was a transition for her from one life to the next. Regan made a plan in her head. She would try it, work toward creating a new life, or she would give up.

Her one alternative was to die. Regan saw limited options. This made sense to her. She hadn't gone as far as to craft the details of a suicide plan, but she considered suicide as a reasonable option. She would move on and try to start fresh, or she would cease to exist. The two options made total sense to her.

Regan opened and read the last card, which was nothing significant. She felt a little let down. There were no big answers to life written on the inside. It contained no quick fix, and offered no explanation for why this tragedy occurred. Nothing would make her child dying seem okay. Nothing would make it understandable. She would never be right with the world. Regan hated everyone who sent cards.

She grabbed her new iPhone from her weathered, brown J Crew shoulder bag. She touched the calendar App with her fingertip. It was Friday. Tuesday afternoon, her belongings—not Noah's stuff, not Grace's stuff—would be delivered to the home she had rented. Nothing of Noah's would arrive, and her two boxes of Grace's memories were safely protected in the back of her car. She thought about where she was heading, to a small, two-bedroom farmhouse in Stockbridge, Massachusetts. The idea of a country house appealed to her. This would be her new house for one year. If she kept reviewing the schedule, it would begin to seem real. There was something concrete about her plan that made her feel less anxious.

"Eggs okay?" The server set down a check near Regan's water glass. "You've hardly touched them."

"Oh, they're great, thanks," Regan responded, careful to avoid giving a reason why her stomach was upset and why eating was a chore these days. She was always one to have a big appetite, never overdoing it, but not afraid to order what she liked. Lately, though, nothing tasted appetizing. Her therapist said it was normal, and Regan was deliberate about making sure she got enough calories, even if she couldn't taste much of anything. "The coffee is great, nice and strong."

"You can pay whenever you're ready. I'm heading home soon, but no rush. The cashier can take you anytime," the waitress said kindly.

"Where's home?" Regan asked, surprising herself.

The waitress was an open book. "Sturbridge, it's not too far. But I gotta head over to Medford to help out my mom. Ever since my dad went on hospice, we've been doing around-the-clock-care, me and my brothers."

"Oh, I see. I'm sorry," Regan said quietly with sympathetic eyes.

The waitress—Bev was her name, according to the stained name tag on her button-down shirt—continues, "Yeah, it's been over a month now, probably has a week or so left, the nurses say. They are real nice. They take care of everything. All we do when we get there is sit by his side, maybe read to him or look at old photo albums. He's not all there, but it helps Mom out and makes us feel useful. Better than a hospital with tubes and that sterile smell. I can't stand that smell, makes me sick."

This is the way it should be, Regan thought. A parent was supposed to die before a child. "Well, I hope he's in good spirits when you get there," Regan added, hoping to avoid any more small talk.

"Where are you from?" the server asked.

"Oh, me? Just passing through."

"Husband? Kids? You married?"

"Nope, not me. Not interested. Not very nurturing either. No kids. I like my space." Regan was confused as to why she answered this way. "Here you go." She handed the waitress exact change and a three-dollar tip. "I'm all set." Then she shuffled the cards into a pile, zipped her purse, and got up to leave. The waitress took this as her cue to move along, untied her apron, and tucked the cash into her front pocket.

"Take care now," she said to Regan.

"You too," she responded.

Regan walked out, depositing the stack of cards and torn envelopes in the trash. She thought about the craziness of the holidays, what a whirlwind the last month had been. Distant relatives asked her to join them for Thanksgiving and Christmas. She declined, making up some excuses that no one dared to question.

Truth was, she stopped visiting family long ago. After Grace was born, she realized just how isolating life was. No deep family ties. Both her parents were gone. Her annual or semi-annual trips less than an hour away to visit Camille and the kids were too infrequent, yet they were the closest thing she had to family, and even those stopped because it was too painful to see the twins, who were the same age as Grace.

She thought marrying Noah would change her. She married Noah for her father. Because it was expected, and it's what he wanted for her. It was the next logical step in her life. Even in marriage, she isolated, keeping his family away with a myriad of excuses. She never had to get too close to the distant relatives. With Noah's work schedule, the family knew he was busy trying to make partner. Once he finally did, people had gotten busy moving on with their own lives, and raising children. This didn't seem to bother Regan. It was her version of normal.

Since Regan's mom had passed when she was a child, she remembered a flurry of activity around the house. It reminded her of the craziness that surrounded the funeral services for Grace. People said they were there if she needed anything. Promises of visits that never happened. People were busy. They went on with their own lives.

Regan didn't resent them. But it taught her about life. She understood. Once she became a mother, she really understood the time and commitment it took to be a parent. Parenting didn't leave much time for keeping up distant relationships. Regan had a way of justifying her lack of effort—they were relatives she didn't really know anyway. She counted the empty promises from the people who didn't come through for her. In order to keep those relationships up, at least one side would need to make an effort.

She didn't like it, but she understood. For years, she thought something was wrong with her. Now she knew that life took over. People were simply busy. It was kind of the way the world worked, her world anyway. And it was okay. She was busy too.

The holiday invitations were obligatory, but out of kindness. She declined them all, choosing a new path. As Regan politely rejected holiday invitations, she knew not much more would come from the relationships in the future. She was okay with this. People appeared relieved when she shared her plan to move out of the Boston area and head toward the Berkshires for a year.

There, no one would know her parents' history or about her recent circumstances. She wasn't the daughter of an alcoholic or the daughter of a cancer victim. There would be no gossip, or whispers at the coffee shop, or concerned glances of pity. She wasn't the daughter of a crazy father. She wasn't the mother of a dead daughter. She wasn't the wife whose husband cheated.

She was Regan.

She drove away from the truck stop into a slow, falling snow. Barely a dusting was made on the road. She turned her headlights on and savored a renewed resilience for getting to the inn. She was ready to get as far away from her old life as she could.

BETH JANNERY

Chapter Eight

A feeling of wonder washed over her, but also dread. Would the inn keeper be home? She better not be chatty. Not a single person knew Regan in the Berkshires. The sophisticated country was unassuming and Yankees tended to not to pry.

Regan arrived at the inn for the weekend, plus a few days, so she could get settled before getting the keys to her temporary house for the year. The inn was inviting. There were no odd doll collections, no menagerie of smelly cats. You never knew what you'd get walking into a small bed and breakfast.

She pulled up to the inn, parked, and entered an unlocked archway still draped with garland, a hint of evergreen in the air. The red plaid bows were crooked and worn. One had fallen down to the blue, cracked, slate underfoot.

Inside, Regan stepped into an almost silent house except for the low NPR Fresh Air jetting out of the back hallway. She could tell immediately it was a warm and comforting well-loved home, a perfect quintessential and understated New England inn with all the charm of a different era.

Peeking in, she saw the hallway lead to a crackled alcove with muddy worn Wellingtons that had a calming effect to her soul. She remembered Grace's colorful kid-sized Wellies. In them, she conquered any puddle in her path.

To her right, she headed toward an old pantry-style mudroom. Thick, solid wood painted with layers of memories. Her room keys, her cookies, and her welcome note were displayed on a tray. A glass of sherry sat waiting to say hello. Regan grabbed the keys marked for her and downed the drink.

Disappearing toward her guest quarters, Regan quickly carried her weekend provisions underarm. She steadily maneuvered the corners of the tight and twisty stairwell. Her upper arm slid against fraying and peeling wallpaper, coming apart at the seams. Almost dropping her bags, she felt an indent forming in her bent fingers. She wouldn't let go until she successfully pushed her heavy room door open, where she unloaded her belongings into a loud pile on the wide-plank wood floor. Her fingers stung; a quarter-inch of tender skin began to rise back to the surface as her blood circulated again. The sensation of not feeling her finger matched the rest of her — numb.

Then, the slight yet consistent pang in her finger jolted her into a yearning to be touched, to feel pain, to feel something. She'd been numb since the accident.

Without unpacking yet or even surveying the modest guest room, Regan's fingers began to unbutton her blouse. The middle buttons were stretched, almost broken, the fabric hugging her swelling breasts. Releasing the shirt, she slid her hand into her bra, directly pinching her ripe nipple, squeezing it with an intense rush that simultaneously shot a sensual warmth between her legs. It felt good to touch skin. Squeezing her inner thigh muscles and lowering her left hand, she eased onto the antique canopy mattress while lowering her fingers, two erect fingers, over her clit. Damp already from quiet thoughts on her country drive, Regan's wetness sweetened. Instantly, her lips moisten and fingers slid in, creating a jolt, a desire to ride her hand fast and hard, momentarily wishing for a stranger to enter her.

Regan instantly came up with a plan, her art of distraction at work. She decided for a weekend adventure. Her rising sensuality would be carried into the night. Wondering who may walk into her life that night, she knew an encounter would meet her need to escape. She must get out of her skin. Nothing too personal, she simply didn't want to think or feel.

In and out a light sleep, Regan stirred, bringing herself back into the late afternoon. Doors slammed shut. Outside her window before looking out, she sensed a rushed couple, weary and argumentative from traffic arriving in tightness, abrupt to each other. She knows it would take an hour or so until they were wrapped near the fire, agreeing how much a weekend at an inn was needed in both their lives. To take time off from work to recharge and also to reconnect. Regan glanced through the yellowed curtain without thinking she'd get caught.

Her peering outside the inn window was noticed by the husband while his wife was organizing the car's contents, reaching for the trunk. In an instant, she observed the man locked in on her — urging a meeting. They stared too long. She broke the three-second rule. Her eyes didn't divert until at least six seconds. They absorbed into each other — the man getting out of the car with New York license plates, and the mysterious long-haired woman in the window. Meanwhile, the woman at the car, obviously annoyed she was the one locking up, distracted herself with her cell, texting and on edge inside, wanting to scream, "Why the hell do I always have to do everything?"

Wondering when the evening would climax, Regan waited the cocktail hour. She saw a sign posted in the foyer at check-in. She imagined the house guests would gather down in the great room; a wine tasting would ease the guests into their Friday night. It was hard to believe she left Boston earlier today. Her plan to close the door on the past started working quickly — new place, new people, new Regan. She readied herself to meet the other weekenders, almost willing them into an experience of seduction and friendship.

Chapter Nine

The late afternoon was spent reading literature, exploring minds, and feeling intimate in a room of strangers. On the one hand, Regan felt too open, vulnerable, exposed, but there was a gentleness at the inn and she was surrounded by art and felt a touch of affection. It was a quiet afternoon to center herself and then to reach out of her comfort zone. Strangers had a way of forcing her to do that.

The wine tasting at the inn passed quickly. Drinks flowed, conversation was easy, everyone was in good spirits, being whoever they wanted to be. Everyone drank more than they should have, especially Regan and Leo. The cocktail hour opened the door to dinner. Regan surprised herself by agreeing to dinner with the strangers, her new weekend friends. Dinner with the New York City couple seemed like a good place to start her new life. She could practice her new part.

She was up to something, but wasn't sure what. They were openly intimate at dinner, this couple. It felt odd to be at an intimate dinner with strangers; nothing a round of sake couldn't cure. "Cheers," the group said in unison. Regan looked around, drinking in the moment—random people in a quiet place, having dinner in town. It was just what she needed, a perfect escape. Two miles away, Canyon Ranch diners counted calories. Regan counted wine glasses. Plenty flowed as they awkwardly eased into the night.

It was time now, the antics began. Leo ordered sake shots for the table, then a personal-size bottle of sake for each person. Regan and Leo drank it like water. No one seemed to pay any attention. The obligatory small talk ended. Leo was distracted and did not listen to his wife as she shared the witty tale he'd heard many times—so many freaking times. It could be up to thirty if he cared enough to count.

Shut the fuck up, he screamed silently. Regan was aware of him. She heard something. She sensed his frustration.

"How did life get this dull?" Leo asked Regan with his eyes from across the table. His wife, Jennifer, and the other guest, a dark-haired poet, were busy exchanging drunken stories and more pleasantries. Leo's eyes rolled. Regan acknowledged it. They bonded.

As Regan expected, Leo came on to her, but in a more exciting way than she imagined. Something probed at her. Yes, it was his hand, an under-the-table cliché, but she invited more. She continued and went along with it.

Why not?

No foreplay, unless you counted small talk. Leo was very forward. It didn't seem real to Regan, that someone would be this obvious. He boldly reached under the table, slid his hand up her leg, his fingers searched, parting her. He fumbled underneath her panties, a petite tight thong, which he had suspected would be underneath the alluring stranger's clothes—he was immediately satisfied. It was satin or silk; he couldn't tell and didn't really care. He gave himself a pat on the back for being right. Not only did he make the correct call on the thong, he also confirmed what he visualized. She was totally bare. He'd heard about this. Two of his buddies who had affairs often brought it up—they loved it. It was new to him—a mound bare and smooth. How he wished he had experienced this earlier.

What could be better? He didn't have an answer.

Shaved, or taken off with laser or wax? Whatever. He didn't really care. But he wanted to run his fingers along her smooth shape. He wanted to explore her wonderland.

A Dave Matthews tune came to mind. Or was it John Mayer? Everyone was drunk now.

He felt between her legs.

This was not the jungle mess his wife grew. With Jennifer, it was like getting lost in the trees—dense, smelly, and too familiar. A humid rainforest he no longer enjoyed. At least these were his most recent memories. He hadn't visited "Australia," as he'd often called it, in quite some time. Sure, she was busy with the little ones, but he felt shunned and rejected. It was as if sex was some sort of reward nowadays, a gold star he could earn if he took out the trash, paid the bills, and remembered to bring home flowers. Doing a quick vacuum would surely get him a quickie. He didn't like that he had to barter for sex with his wife.

God, he heard himself and knew he sounded like an ass. But didn't he deserve something on the side after years of the same grind? Plus, there were kids now, twins actually, who sucked the life out of his wife. They took all her attention. That's when she'd left him. He thought back to a better time when the Sunday paper and Starbucks in bed was a tradition. That was when gourmet coffee was innovative and people knew what it was to get ink on their fingertips. Then, one day, it all changed. He wasn't even second fiddle; it was more like third or fourth. One step before the dog, and that was on a good day. Things changed, he rationalized, as he continued to gently stroke Regan under the table.

At dinner in town, Leo justified his actions; he didn't question them. Not once did he stop to think about a consequence. No, he had to experience her bareness for himself. Just this once, and in went his finger.

Regan didn't budge. In fact, she continued to hold his wife's eye contact and appeared to listen to her boring dialogue. Leo coughed; he cleared his throat after he drank a deep swig of his newly ordered vodka martini. He imagined what he could do to her if they were alone.

Maybe she'd let him in tonight, if he knocked quietly. He'd tell Jennifer he was restless, couldn't sleep, and needed some air. It was plausible. There was an oversized porch where he could claim he visited to gaze at the stars and inhale the unadulterated Berkshires air. In reality, he'd be in Regan's bed, inside her, the woman from the window earlier this afternoon, the woman he was now fingering at the local sushi restaurant.

How was a woman this moist? He hardened, assuming she was damp because of him. A proud moment, and one he would not soon forget. The table got quiet when Regan looked his way. He wasn't caught. No, whew, it was the owner of the restaurant behind him greeting the customers.

Regan was thankful for the oversized, white table cloth that draped down her legs.

Still, she looked his way while she eased her body forward, sliding farther down his finger. Leo imagined the sensation of Regan taking in his shaft and riding him. He took the risk of adding a second finger. She liked it and took it again. This time, he was more forceful. She knew he'd be rough with her, which was what she wanted — to go further out of her mind. She craved a pleasure with no choices or demands. Pure sex at the grip of a stranger; who was she now? A brief thought of Noah and the bitch came to mind, but Regan deliberately and instantly pushed it away.

Jennifer chimed in.

"It's amazing, really, to meet a random guest at an inn and to feel such a connection."

Regan nodded with guilty hesitation. The touching stopped. Jennifer included the studious-looking man next to her. Regan met him at the inn earlier, but had ignored him. What use was he to her? He blended into the background. Regan nicknamed him "the poet." She had nicknames for everyone.

"I mean, Leo and I were so frazzled just trying to get out of the city," Jennifer went on. "We almost didn't drop the kids at my mother's penthouse. Driving all the way out here seemed so far after an insane week."

"Insane," she repeated herself.

This is insane. I'm getting off by someone I just met. Regan shifted in her seat.

Then Jennifer listed her to-do list for the day, telling Regan just how exhausted she was from running around after the twins. "Do you have kids?"

I don't know you. I don't care. But your husband was just finger-fucking me. Regan kept her thoughts to herself. "No, I don't have kids. Single, never married. Like it that way." Regan grabbed the attention of the waiter and ordered another round, successfully dodging any fire line of questioning that was about to come her way. "A toast." Regan held up her glass and smiled. She was perfecting the art of distraction.

Chapter Ten

God, how could I be so cold? It was a little nugget of truth about who Regan was; she could be brutal. Why hadn't she explored this side before? She was accustomed to always doing the right thing, acting properly and behaving as a lady should.

The chit-chat wound down. Leo had slowly removed himself from Regan's smooth lips. They were all drunk on sake, and martinis, and wine. She knew this was no excuse.

What was it about the forbidden that excited her? It was clearly wrong. Desire. Was it an emotion or a feeling? Didn't matter much now. What's done was done, and she wanted more.

Now a million miles away from her old life, she knew to savor the night.

She was caught off guard, feeling shame, sadness, and even some guilt—but not as much remorse as she thought she should. Jennifer was once a beautiful woman. She'd really let herself go. Part of Regan felt sorry for her, the other part felt resentment over her two children. She wanted what she had. The other part was plain annoyance. *Shut up,* Regan wanted to scream. His wife talked incessantly.

But down deep, Regan didn't want to hurt anyone. She knew she should put a stop to Leo's advances.

Jennifer was nice enough and suspected nothing. She should not have let herself go. Complacency killed. It was his desire for something new. That was all. Nothing was wrong with Jennifer.

The moment hurt. Regan's memory rushed in. All that time of feeling angry at the other woman who came between her and Noah. The moment also helped. She realized his decision to stray wasn't about her. It was about Noah. The affair was about him and what he lacked inside. He was void of any integrity or character. But no matter how Regan dissected it, the affair changed her. It left her empty. And Noah ended up with the bitch. Regan lost everything. Life was never what you expected.

"Let's drink to life not being what you expect." Regan interrupted the small dinner party with another toast. Glasses clinked.

The waiter added water glasses to the table. There were always wet circles on wood.

She deliberately looked down at her plate. Her fingers ran along the tip of her empty sake glass. He stopped touching her and she remained with her eyes diverted until the check came. Still, she could feel the weight of his stare, and it excited her.

Before they left the Japanese restaurant, she lifted her eyes. This time, she turned to the poet. His literary wit, which at first charmed her, began to bore her. He tried too hard. Still, she knew he'd figure into the sensuality of the weekend at the inn. She turned her attention to him. She knew better than to continue with Leo, the married man. Surely, Jennifer would catch on and Regan simply had too much of a conscience for that. She couldn't imagine playing the role of the other woman, even though she had allowed his hands to seduce her for a majority of the dinner. She drew her line in the sand.

Regan began listening to the poet. She would find out more. What was she doing now? What game was she playing? The dinner party headed back to the inn. It was a short walk from the town green, and everyone was getting tired. They decided to call it a night. Leo and Jennifer said goodnight and closed their door; the poet walked Regan to her door and invited himself in. Regan didn't know what game they were playing, but she decided to go along. She enjoyed playing a new role and was curious to see where it would lead.

She soon discovered the poet was firm with her. He got off on it. His intensity came as a pleasant surprise. He directed her body against the inn wall, in her bedroom, late at night when they all stumbled home. By now, Leo and Jennifer might be asleep. Most likely, Leo was lying on his back, wide-eyed, awake and irritated. Jennifer rolled away when Leo climbed in. His advances were denied; she claimed to be too tired. It was true, he knew this, but it pissed him off.

Regan was glad the poet shut up, finally. She liked finding out there was more to him. A role play began. He started to force her, sort of, something she never could have predicted. He told her what to do. He pinned her arms above her head, held her wrists with one hand while his belt fell to the floor. With his zipper down, he tugged at his cock and worked it into her, almost too much for her to take. She gasped and was somewhere else. Nowhere.

Gone. He gave her orders and she obeyed. The scenario was perfect. Her lips parted and she took him in, again and again, as Leo listened from two doors down.

Chapter Eleven

He left. The poet's real name was Jack. She wanted him to go. She released, finished him off, and couldn't be bothered to cuddle. Once, after Noah moved out, she had a one-night-stand. Why did people call it that? Who was standing? She didn't care to stay the night. All it did for her was relieve her of some pain, temporarily. It helped her to forget.

She heard the man, whose name she didn't care to remember, say, "You're like a man. You're the perfect woman. A body of curves, a sharp mind, and you don't want to wake up in the morning next to the person you screwed."

No, I'd rather be alone. Regan kept her thoughts to herself.

Now, more than ever, Regan was alone. And she learned, from the poet, that she fucked like a man. It made sense—rushed, physical, detached, focused—she could use people. The feeling empowered her; it also made her painfully sad.

Sometimes, in the quiet of the night, once the day had settled, she heard the darkness. It screamed at her, a lonely roar. If she wasn't careful, she started to listen to it; otherwise, she found some distraction—sex, chocolate, reading, wine—and it dimmed to a low moan. Or it disappeared.

But it never stayed away, and tonight, Regan heard it. The relief of the stranger only lasted for so long. He left her raw. Too short for a retreat, it was in the space in between actions and thoughts, where she was most vulnerable.

Tonight, she couldn't drown it out. It'd been said that truth lived in this space. It was what was real when the rest of life fell aside. It was the most uncomfortable place for Regan. Finally, sleep came. It was that deep morning sleep where the dreams roamed and fears ran free.

Regan stirred, rolled over, and smiled. She felt Grace's small hand in hers, warm and innocent. Suddenly, Regan sat straight up. She looked around the room, saw the canopy and the dressing table and her luggage in the corner. Her camisole on the floor in a sad bunch. She remembered now.

Had she fallen asleep?

What was that? A dream, or had Grace visited her? This had only happened one other time since her death, and Regan waited for her again each night, always disappointed when she'd wake with a longing. Sweet Grace.

Sweet, sweet Grace.

I'm so sorry.

Or she wouldn't wake because she hadn't slept one wink; insomnia settled in early after "that night." It was a time she pushed deep into the bowels of her mind. Regan knew what she was doing. It was her protective blanket to be washed and laundered and ironed for another day.

Regan's therapist reminded her sensations could only stay hidden for so long. Regan knew demons remained dormant for some time. But she knew the ugly would come. She would face life alone without Grace, without Noah, without certainty.

She felt her eyes get heavy again; she stretched like a cat under the one hundred percent Egyptian duvet. Her restlessness gave way to the softness. The night stood still for her even as the morning light came in. She felt protected. It was as if the visit from Grace gave her peace. Maybe it was a drunken hallucination; Regan was well aware she'd be hung over in the daylight.

Her to-do list popped in her head.

Ugh, reality? Not yet. *Please, no.* Regan tried to push it aside and fall back asleep, but her task list kept scrolling.

She counted on her fingers while lying back down: Sunday, Monday, Tuesday—a few more days before the moving truck showed up. She made a mental note to go online and fill out the change of address form, something she wanted to avoid until the very last minute. Soon, she would turn the key into the door of the old farmhouse she rented.

Regan knew she was lucky to find a place. She continued to count and plan. She calculated once the month ended, the boxes would be unpacked.

She got through the fucking holidays and she had to arrive, and soon enough, unpack and bury herself in work.

She ached to feel her small hands once more. Planning for any tomorrow without Grace felt wrong.

Finally, she slept. When the sleep came it helped.

She dreamed of the poet. And of the husband who should have remained off limits.

Sex was a temporary fix. It filled a void.

A useful distraction, until it stopped working.

Chapter Twelve

Jennifer jumped up from the breakfast table.

"I bet I know someone who needs coffeeeeeeee." Jennifer's voice belonged in a cheery Disney movie. Maybe Snow White. Regan rolled her eyes.

"Oh my God, Regan, I'm on, like, my third cup of Joe."

People who called coffee *Joe* or *Java* annoyed Regan.

"Wow, aren't you perky." Regan shook her head, forcing a cordial smile.

Regan wasn't perky. She didn't like people who tried too hard. She didn't like morning small talk.

She had to admit Jennifer was somewhat likeable even if she was perky. If Regan could somehow peel away Jennifer's dense layers of marriage and motherhood, a more likeable woman might emerge.

Likeable might be too strong a word.

Regan did notice Jennifer's breasts were also perky. Regan couldn't get away without wearing a bra. Regan played with nicknames for Perky. *Jenni* or *Jen Jen*. Jennifer didn't seem to fit.

Jen Jen had erect nipples this morning. Hard not to notice. She hadn't hidden them under a turtleneck and wool sweater. Why the fitted J Crew jersey today? It was a very different look from last night when she had seemed so uptight. Rigid even. She went from being dull and boring, annoying even, to perky — and still annoying.

Regan imagined Leo having sex with Jen Jen before breakfast. Her high-beams were lit. That must be what happened.

Geez, tangent! Regan often got lost in her own thoughts. It had been happening more frequently, since Grace died.

Gotta get the hell out of here. Regan was careful not to show her aggravation on her face. She gulped down a quick bite and planned her exit.

She noticed Leo and the poet were chatty. Jack kept looking over to smile. Leo may have, but Regan was oblivious to him. Once she shut the door on an affair in her mind, there was no revisiting the idea. Could men be chatty? She wondered.

Small talk continued around the room. Quiet classical music filled the background. In the forefront, there hung a fog of lust, mystery, and deceit. It would have been palpable to anyone who joined the morning meal, but only three of the five guestrooms were occupied. There were rumblings of some well-known author making his way to the inn, but Regan only heard parts of conversations.

There must be a hidden corner where the two could duck out later after Leo fed Jennifer some drinks. His mind ran wild. He'd finally have time alone with Regan. He'd show her what she had missed. Leo didn't like getting played. He didn't like coming in last, as he did at home.

Regan was oblivious to his scheming. He was the furthest thought in her mind.

"Cranberry-orange or scone?" The perky interruption broke her daze.

"Huh?"

"Do you want a muffin or a scone?" Jen Jen blurted in Regan's direction.

She's at it again. Regan was careful not to roll her eyes.

Was she always this talented at breaking into conversation? The limelight didn't suit her. Attention getter. Hadn't anyone taught her that less is more?

Regan realized she was hungry.

"Is there anything low carb?" Regan asked to no one in particular.

Jen Jen winced. A wave of insecurity flushed her face. Maybe she should be eating low carb too. Geez, Miss Perfect over there. Perfect skin, shiny hair, and expensive yoga pants. She knew the type. Jen Jen pushed the green feeling away, silently cursing her husband for not making partner and not bringing in the salary he promised. How were they going to pay for private schooling in the city? New York preschool waiting lists were miles long. She did her best to save, to buy fake designer, though she knew the fabric always looked cheap. She wouldn't buy the expensive yoga pants. She loathed Regan for the way she looked and for the life she led. The irony was she didn't know her life at all.

Jen Jen drew in a deep breath and walked toward Regan. What was it about this woman that intrigued Jennifer? She extended her arm, handed Regan a plate, and pointed to the buffet. Before Jennifer pulled her hand away, she felt a sudden urge, a sensation of being drawn to Regan. Then, slowly, Regan let go of the plate. Her fingertips traced along the top of Regan's hand. She blushed. Her hand was free.

It was an odd encounter.

What had Jennifer done? She looked away. She wondered what had come over her. Had she really done that? Yes, she flirted. It was something she would have done to a man she was attracted to, had she not been married, of course. Jennifer never strayed; she always did the right thing. She had to admit to herself there was something sensual about Regan — the way she looked, or her confidence, or the way she drew the men into conversations. It should make Jennifer jealous and uneasy toward Regan, but it began to pull Jennifer into Regan's seduction. Except Regan didn't know she was seducing anyone other than perhaps the poet and married Leo, although she had already discarded them both.

The guys waved a hello in Regan's direction. The poet raised his coffee mug. Breakfast was continental, as Jen Jen pointed out. Doing without the formality pleased Regan. She was off and running for her big day of relaxing. Odd how a woman could keep busy trying to fit everything in so she could "take it easy." She reviewed her checklist: R&R, spa, meditate, and time set aside for journaling. *It sort of defeats the purpose*, she thought. *There is something odd about scheduled relaxation time.*

Regan got to the end of her mental list and stared at her plate. What had that been? She replayed the exchange with Jen Jen. She played it again in her mind. It surprised her. She hadn't expected a move like that from Jen Jen. From the men, perhaps, but not from the tightly wound woman from New York.

This could be fun. Regan toyed with the idea. She looked up. She was grateful people were not deeply engaging in conversation this morning. She wasn't ready for a round of questions.

She deliberately stared at Jennifer. She caught her gaze and held on to it. If anything was to happen, it would be Regan's first encounter like this, with a woman. There was no doubt it was new to Jen Jen.

Jennifer took notice of Regan's gaze. She did the up and down eye thing. A woman knew how to give it well. To show interest, they looked across the room, then looked down and then back up, finishing with a coy, slight smile. It worked on men. No reason it wouldn't work for women too.

Regan caught herself. She had fun doing this to Jennifer. Or was Jennifer doing it to her? Hard to tell how it started, but it was there. Maybe there was something about Jennifer's peachy-rose lips after all. Why hadn't she seen them at the sushi restaurant? Jennifer got nervous, looked away, and finished the muffin. Her mouth was dry; she placed the mimosa to her mouth and swallowed. Yes, Regan thought, it was her lips. She was drawn to her lips. Regan went back to reading the newspaper at her table, even though she knew it was slightly rude and antisocial. It was a layer of protection. She read the same three paragraphs several times.

She wasn't sure where that flirtation came from. Normally, Regan wasn't attracted to women, and certainly not someone as vanilla as Leo's wife. Regan played with it; she finished eating, got up, and turned toward the door. She pulled an oversized poncho over her head. Her body, even under the cape was curvy. She tugged on her Uggs. Covered and warm, her neck still looked slender and the outline of her collar bones sexy. She wrapped her scarf around her thin neck. She liked the tightness as she pulled it.

Being somewhat obvious, Regan turned back and eyed Jen Jen.

No one could miss it.

Regan waved.

"Bye, guys, I'm off to the spa. Have a great day. Maybe I'll see you by the fire later." With that, Regan was out the door.

Hint, hint.

This was a statement more than a question. She liked directing. She hoped Jennifer would be by the fire later. Perhaps, they could share some red wine.

"Bye," they said in stereo. Everyone was off to do their own thing. It was a restful Saturday, just what the weekend was for.

The door closed. It got quiet, then their conversation moved to other topics. What time the snow was expected. Where the best bookstore was located. Was the pub in town all locals or would they be welcome? Things like that. It was nice to think about something other than kids, home, work, and Regan. The buzz of the champagne warned Jennifer's skin. The day held possibility.

Jennifer wondered if what she'd seen was real. Had Regan given her the look? Jennifer didn't like the idea of being with another woman. It grossed her out; she lived a basic sexual existence, not venturing out of the norm.

But what was normal?

Sex to Jennifer was for making babies or fulfilling marital duties. Jennifer wondered where she fell on the sexual scale—she was always an extreme. Was she an uptight, rigid nun, or a secretly slutty girl with a desire to role play? Certainly, she couldn't be the latter. Maybe she was a little of both?

The thought of a woman kissing another woman always repulsed her. Yuck, only once did she respond to it, long ago, but all girls who were coming of age experimented. Breast buds were touched, pushed on, and cupped. To have the thought cross her mind now, as a mom and wife, it was unthinkable.

She felt her panties get wet. This caught her off guard. Would Leo notice? Jennifer was the kind of woman who avoided mirrors when she was naked. If she ever looked, she'd see her curves were sexy, and if she could learn to use her body, to move her body the right way, she might enjoy being dusted off.

She thought about sex all day. It was a long day. The quickie in the morning light didn't do much to satisfy Jennifer.

Regan was off at *The Healing Place,* getting centered and paying to be touched. There was nothing like a massage. She wouldn't owe a thing. It wasn't reciprocal. Nothing was expected. Only the fee and a tip and she could leave.

Chapter Thirteen

The massage table was warmed and the room smelled of Johnson's Baby Powder. Twenty minutes into the hour-long-deep-tissue-massage, Regan finally relaxed. She gave into the weekend at the inn even more. As she enjoyed the intense touch, and listened to the lulling, meditative music, her mind wandered. She saw such sweetness. Jennifer stood before her, right there in the massage room. Regan was alert enough to know this was not real, but she was not dreaming.

Regan tried to push the unwelcome idea of Jennifer out of her mind. She conjured up unflattering images. Regan noticed Jennifer's jeans seemed a bit too tight this morning. She had a few extra baby pounds. But she was real, and the idea of teasing Jennifer intrigued her.

The seduction of the massage continued. The massage therapist was completely professional, but Regan's mind drifted. She eased into the fantasy. She knew how it might unfold. Regan wouldn't let Jennifer's panties go past her thighs. She wanted to watch Jennifer get aroused the way Regan had as a school girl the first time she got fingered.

Regan thought about teaching Jennifer how to move, how to take both her hands and, using her own fingers, spread open her lips so Leo could lay his tongue on her underused private area.

Maybe she'd talk dirty to her, see how far she could push her boundaries.

She heard someone talking.

"Did that feel good? Are you relaxed now? How was it? Did I go too deep?" The massage therapist wanted to know how Regan enjoyed her session.

Regan stirred, moaned quietly. The voice got louder.

Regan was confused. She opened her eyes. The massage therapist announced the end to the session. "Oh, that was great. I must have drifted off. Thanks so much."

"Be sure to drink a couple eight ounce glasses of water. Get up slowly," the therapist instructed.

Regan was disappointed. Her fantasy was interrupted. Damn, just when it was getting good.

She must have dozed off. She couldn't remember the last time she wasn't tired. Life was catching up to her. She could no longer outrun it.

Chapter Fourteen

Darkness seemed to fall much earlier in this New England town. When Regan left the spa, the air had turned sharp and brisk. Her wrap was not enough, but she smelled woody smoke and knew the inn's fire was burning. Fortunately, the massage center was not far from the inn; Regan counted her paces and noted the sun's disappearance.

She turned the metal knob, shook off the cold, and made herself at home. There was a buzz in the atmosphere—the house felt vibrant. She heard voices, more than expected, coming from down the hall. Maybe there was a reception?

She remembered the inn often invited locals in for drinks—it wasn't an official happy hour, but it was a meeting place of sorts. Gerta had mentioned something about it. She told Regan not to be concerned if she saw a group of people on Saturday evening because they gathered for cocktails, held an informal discussion, and made their way off into town to The Heritage Tavern, the local pub. For the foodies, there were a couple of bistros that blessed the landscape, a French café, and some fusion cooking place she couldn't recall the name.

Ah, she said to herself, *now the new quote makes sense.* Gerta was always changing the readings in the foyer, which were placed thoughtfully on a music stand at the stairs' lower landing. Regan stood in the entryway and read the latest posted literature, attributed to André Lorde.

"The sharing of joy, whether physical, emotional, psychic, or intellectual, forms a bridge between the sharers which can be the basis for understanding much of what is not shared between them, and lessens the threat of their difference."

"Hello?" Gerta called out in her now familiar accent.

Leo stood up as self-appointed greeter, as if to say, "Don't get up, Gerta. I'll get the door."

Regan stalled. She stood still reading Lorde. She wanted so much to slink into the hot shower, come out refreshed without anyone catching her. Their eyes met. Leo must have sensed her pull and invited her to join them "later" for a drink.

"Oh, I'm staying in tonight, but thank you, Leo." She sounded so proper.

"Here, I mean a drink here at the inn." Leo pointed back toward the room filled with socializing. "Here, in the study."

A cork popped in the back room. At the sound, Regan smiled.

"Oh, okay, sure, sounds fun! Let me go clean up," she answered.

Leo leaned toward her. "I'd offer to help you. In fact, I'd love to wash you — or watch you wash," he stammered. "But, well, you know."

"Yes, I know." Regan shrugged.

"The wife," they said in hushed unison.

"Yeah, about that," Regan continued, thankful they had an uninterrupted moment. "I feel a bit awkward about what happened. You have to know that isn't like me." She was genuinely remorseful.

His smile dropped. "But isn't it?"

She looked puzzled. Then it hit her. He must know about Jack.

"Just drop it. I'm sorry. You're right. It was spontaneous, sexy as hell, and I'll pretend it never happened if you will." He extended his hand.

"Thanks for the memories?" Regan played along.

"Deal?" he asked.

"Deal," she agreed, anxious to end this exchange. They shook on it.

He felt the coldness of her palm against his warm hand. How she drew him in. He was captivated. He looked at her closely; her eyes seemed tired but beautiful. Her skin fresh and clean, smooth. So close he could touch her cheek.

"Leo?" a voice called out.

"Yes, dear?" A note of sarcasm entered his voice, accompanied by a quick eye roll for Regan's benefit.

They dropped hands and agreed that Regan would come down to join the fun, nothing more—an unspoken understanding. Leo turned and walked back to the crowd.

Regan was about to run up the stairs to shower when Jen Jen turned the corner.

"Hey."

"Shit," Regan mumbled. "Oh, hey. I'm a mess. Just back from the spa. I'm going to change. Meet you for a drink in a few, if that's okay?" Regan was surprised at how pretty Jen looked tonight.

"You look great," Jen added. "I love your Yoga pants."

Regan looked down, saw how they clung to her thighs. She pulled her cape over her head and moved forward, taking it off directly in front of Jen. "Cool, I'll be down in a bit."

Jennifer watched her. Regan's hair pulled out of the ponytail and fell into a thousand strands; her top went up a few inches as she took off her wrap, baring her midriff. Jen looked at her waist, her hips, and up her chest, noticing her breasts and hair.

"Okay then. Uh, yeah, see you," Jen said.

"Okay," Regan shouted from halfway up the stairs. "Hey, pour me a B&B, will you? I need to warm up." She made sure Jen saw her smile.

Jen caught it. How could she miss it? She was looking for it, for a sign, searching for anything. Good, she thought, this morning she hadn't imagined the exchange. She was anxious all day anticipating another encounter.

Leo heard Regan call down from the stairs, placing her drink order.

"I'll get it," Leo jumped in, without thinking. The couple was standing in study now, looking at the bottles set out on the dry sink.

"No." Jen motioned with her hand to stop Leo from reaching for a glass. "I've got it. She looked so cold," Jen said, deflecting the conversation, taking control of it. "I think it's really going to start coming down, the snow. Don't you think?"

Leo responded, being sure to agree. "Yeah, snow, a lot of it," he said as his thoughts turned to worry. He backed off.

"Here, let me pour the drink." She nudged her husband away from the small antique bar as he was reaching for a bottle. "I'll run it up to her," she insisted, giving him a knowing glance.

Leo wasn't going to argue. He didn't want to be obvious. He couldn't let his wife see his attraction to Regan. He hoped she didn't already suspect.

He immediately backed down.

Smart man.

Chapter Fifteen

Jennifer diverted her eyes. Strange, he thought, for some reason she looked guilty. He watched her hands tremble as she poured the brandy from the dark bottle. She bit her lower lip, very aware Leo was next to her. He watched her closely now. It began to click. Their eyes met. She looked down at the full glass of B&B to her mouth, inhaled slowly, and sipped. The alcohol warmed her lips. It burned. Leo slid his hand around her back and pulled her close to him, against him. He kissed her seductively. The room, still full, took notice.

He allowed himself to believe that Jennifer may be attracted to Regan. He hoped. It would be incredible, every man's fantasy. It was clear now what Jennifer was doing. She was flirting with Regan, or the idea of her. He chose not to speak and waited in anticipation, hoping he was not imagining this.

Still, he worried this was all an act. Was she up to something? Had she caught him touching Regan under the table Friday night? Leo pushed the thought out of his head. He knew Jennifer enough to know she would have said something immediately. She would have been pissed.

But her interest in Regan surprised him. Married to a woman for years, how could there be anything left to discover? His worry switched to arousal. Leo thought of his wife's stained lips touching Regan's skin. How sexy it would be. Maybe he didn't know his wife after all.

He wondered how well anyone really knew anyone. Jennifer walked past him.

Jennifer was almost at Regan's door now. Leo refilled his glass, paused for a long moment, and joined the poet and of few of the locals near the bookshelves. They talked snow and weather and wind chill factors. Leo didn't hear any of it.

Someone commented about the background music — Tchaikovsky. Igor Markevich was the conductor of the London Symphony Orchestra. A self-appointed classical expert in the room named it. "Symphony No. 5 in E minor." The room quieted. The sounds of the symphony grew louder. It was as if the conductor tapped his baton on the mantle. *Click, clack, click.*

Beautiful.

"I believe Tchaikovsky wrote this while at the edge of an emotional breakdown," someone in the corner rattled on. "I believe it was during his first marriage."

Another voice added, "Yes, but isn't that true of all marriage? First or second, someone is always on the verge of a breakdown."

There was uncomfortable laughter. Then, a toast, glasses raised, taking the edge off. "Yes, cheers, a toast to marriage," someone said.

"Or lack thereof," another man laughed.

It was an odd group, awkward but honest. *Clang, clang.* A few more cheers. Several more toasts. Another round.

The music really is lovely, Jennifer thought. She was at Regan's door now. The sounds from downstairs filled the second floor too. Music filled the air. Music and something else. But what? Jennifer couldn't quite put her finger on it. And then she placed her right hand knuckles on Regan's door and knocked three short knocks.

"Come in," Regan called from the bathroom. "I'll be out in a minute."

Jennifer thought it odd Regan's inn door was unlocked. But she wasn't surprised. Nor was she surprised when Regan told her to come in. *Does she know it's me?* Jennifer wondered.

"It's Jennifer," she leaned toward the open bathroom door so Regan could hear her.

"I know," Regan replied. "I'm almost finished. Just hang out for a bit."

It was quiet, except for the running water. Jennifer felt awkward and uncomfortable. Regan must have sensed her unease.

"I had a feeling you might come up," she said.

"You did? What do you mean?" Jennifer asked.

"I can't hear you. The shower, it's too loud. Be out in a second." Regan hurried.

How did she know I might come up here? Jennifer felt like she was caught in the act.

She looked around the room, taking it all in, inhaling Regan's essence. Stacks of books, pages of folded newspapers lay on the bed—almost everything has been read. A journal, pens, heels, perfume, scarves, and a rose-colored bra and panties were placed across the chair. She shouldn't be in here. What is it about this woman? How curious she was. Who was this single woman, out in the world on her own? No kids? Was she independently wealthy? Why wasn't she tied down? Jennifer imagined the possibilities. Her thoughts raced nonsensically. She fantasized about what a glamorous life Regan must lead — no dependence on a man, no twins, no husband who didn't notice her.

Jennifer created stories about Regan, how amazing her life must be. Maybe she was a wanderer. Maybe she wrote for a travel magazine and her only responsibility was meeting a deadline. Or she was a trust fund girl without a worry in the world. Her bills always managed to get paid. Jennifer didn't know. She was fantasizing about a woman's life she hardly knew.

There it was. Jennifer said it to herself. *I have an intense attraction for a woman who flirted with my husband.*

The water turned off. "Hey, I brought you a drink," Jennifer blurted out awkwardly. "I brought your drink," she repeated.

"I heard you, thanks. Bring it in," Regan responded with quiet confidence. Regan heard Jen Jen enter the bathroom. "Thanks. What I was saying was I had a feeling it would be you." Regan paused. "I hoped anyway."

Jennifer stood still, frozen almost.

"Just set it down on the sink," Regan added, trying to put her at ease.

The steam build-up was like a cloud puff, not quite a steam room, but close.

Jennifer did as she was told. She walked a few more paces into the bathroom, the air humid and steamy. The mirror and shower glass were both fogged, but she could see the silhouette of Regan's curvy body outlined behind the glass. It was blurry, but Jennifer saw the fullness of Regan's breasts. She saw her bend over slightly and dry one leg and then the other.

"Jennifer?"

"I'm right here," Jennifer answered. "Your drink is right here." Before Jennifer could set it down, Regan stepped out of the glass shower, her towel in one hand by her side. The other hand reached for the cocktail.

"Thanks," Regan said, smiling. She swallowed. The liquid heat slipped down and she took another sip. Jennifer watched her uncomfortably. But she couldn't look away. They were alone now, nothing between them but thick air and an unspoken something.

"Well, I thought you might want it, the drink. I guess I'll see you downstairs?" Jennifer turned to walk away, her eyes still on Regan's skin—her neck was so smooth she wanted to reach out and touch it. She almost did, but instead, she turned abruptly.

"Where are you going?" Regan kind of laughed. She saw Jennifer's hesitation. "Get back here," she said playfully. "Just hang out with me. Let me throw something on, do my makeup, and head down with you. Besides, we'll probably hear the same stories the guys told the night before."

They both laughed. "Typical," Jennifer responded.

It was a risk for Regan to bring up Leo, but she did so in a way to show more interest in Jennifer than in her husband.

Jennifer smiled. "God, it's so true. After years of hearing the same stories, I've lost count. Are men that predictable?"

"Pretty much." Regan rolled her eyes. They both nodded in agreement. Jennifer stayed and Regan continued to talk to her from the bathroom. Jennifer half listened. Her mind stepped back in time to the first sex scene she'd read as a girl. She looked at Regan's polished

91

toes standing on the thick bathroom rug. She remembered feeling wet and confused after reading the passage about a teenage couple coming of age.

The boy in the novel named his penis Ralph. The girl practiced chest and arm exercises with her girlfriends at sleepovers – *"We must, we must, we must increase our bust."* Over and over the girls would do this and then drop to a giggle. Jennifer remembered her own girlfriends sharing these racy pages of the Judy Blume novel *Forever*.

The teenage couple in the novel ended up having sex. Maybe it was their first time, or her first time, and after he came, the girl felt alone and in awe. She lost her virginity on the bathroom floor.

She clearly remembered the line in the book, *"We made love on the bathroom rug."* She hadn't forgotten it. But she had forgotten the feeling of the new rush of sensuality. It shot through her like a warm wave.

Being here with Regan, seeing her ripe body, Jen had a flow of wetness. She felt the same way as she had back then reading the dirty book.

Regan's pink nail polish was pretty, Jennifer noticed, allowing her eyes to trace Regan's ankle, calf, leg, thigh, and then she felt caught.

Regan looked up at her. She began to dry her body with a thick, white terrycloth towel. She stood on the bathroom rug, but dripped on the old tile floor.

"So, how was your day?" Regan asked.

Jennifer backed farther away from the bathroom and into the bedroom, still watching Regan dry and lotion herself. Regan seemed to invite in the flirtation as the warmth and tingle of the liquor set in.

Just then, Jennifer made a quick decision. *Oh fuck it,* she said to herself. She stopped and deliberately stared at

Regan. Whatever might happen, she'd let happen. She, for once, said what she was thinking.

"Can I just say you have an awesome body? Seriously, you have curves in all the right places. I know that must sound totally weird to say. I'm embarrassed, must be the alcohol." They both laughed.

"Really? Thanks. I'm glad you noticed." Regan enticed her to continue. "You know, you might be in this super mom role right now, and I totally respect that, but I have a feeling you have this hidden something going on. You should show it more, you know what I mean?"

Jennifer didn't know what she meant. "Please, you don't have to be nice. I know I'm not toned, and I've let the twins take over my life. It's funny, Leo used to call my breasts 'the twins.' Then they turned into this feeding machine and my old life began to disappear."

"I think I get it." Regan began getting dressed after brushing out her hair and moisturizing. The room smelled fragment and feminine.

"I miss this—girlfriend time. I mean, I know we hardly know each other, but you are so easy to talk to. Anyway, so tell me about your day." Jennifer stopped talking and listened.

"I miss it too, the girlfriend time." Regan had a way of putting her at ease. "Okay, so my day? Well, it was peaceful," Regan said. She told Jennifer about the spa and the massage. "It's been a long time since I let myself relax like that," Regan shared, catching herself, careful to put the focus back onto Jennifer. "What about you?"

Jennifer continued with the small talk. They went on about the days, compared notes, and Regan finished getting dressed. She handed Jennifer her drink.

"Here, have a sip. Finish it."

"Oh no, too strong for me." Jennifer held up her white wine glass. "I'm a wine drinker." She didn't admit that she'd taken a huge gulp of the brandy before knocking a few minutes earlier.

"Well then, how about a toast?" Regan suggested. "Let's see, how 'bout to new friends? To girlfriends." Regan walked toward her dressed in a v-neck sweater and skinny jeans. Her socks were pink and fluffy.

"Cute socks," Jennifer said, looking down. Were they flirting? She wondered.

Regan laughed. "Thanks." She came closer, clearly into Jennifer's personal space. "Cheers then, to new friends."

"Yeah, here's to girlfriends," Jennifer joined in. "And to lots of brandy and wine."

"And to meeting strangers at strange inns," Regan continued. Glasses clanked.

Jennifer pulled back and sat on the edge of the bed. Regan stayed in her personal space. She noticed it was too close and it made Jennifer squirm. Regan didn't move. She knew what she was doing. She knew she had the control, knew she hadn't imagined the eye contact and the glances. She liked the way it made her feel. Sure, maybe she messed around with Leo and felt some guilt about that, but she knew Jen Jen didn't have a clue. Except for a few missed opportunities in college, Regan hadn't been with a woman. She knew she wasn't a lesbian, or even bi, but bi-curious perhaps. She decided to play with it and sensed Jennifer's "fuck it" attitude tonight. It was worth a try, and exhilarating to step out of her familiar world and be at an inn with strangers where no one knew about Grace or the accident or the divorce.

"So, you really like my socks?" Regan probed.

"Yeah, I really like your socks," Jennifer answered.

"Anything else? Tell me, what else do you like?" Regan asked seductively.

Jennifer caught on, still looking down. "Stop, you know what I said before. I'm embarrassed."

"What? What did you say before? Tell me. Tell me again. You said you liked my curves? You did, no?" Regan was on a roll.

Smiling now, Jennifer said, "I said that...that I liked your... Okay, I said you have a great body. You do."

"Thank you. Tell me again. Say it." Regan took control. "Look at me and say it." She reached over touching Jennifer's hair, stroking it slowly. "Tell me what you like. I want to hear you say it. Don't worry, it's just us."

"Okay," Jennifer continued slowly. "I saw you in the shower when I came in. I watched you."

"I know. I know you were watching," Regan said.

"So, I guess I like your shape. And you have great skin." Jennifer seemed less shy.

"What else? You liked when I bent over? Did you watch me then?" Now Regan felt like Jack, the poet, and she enjoyed leading the seduction.

Regan was taking cues from the poet from last night. She sensed that Jennifer wouldn't act on this playfulness unless Regan directed her. She felt this rush, warmth between her legs. Without thinking, she reached for Jen's hand and led it to her mound. She unzipped her jeans and pushed Jen's hand against her skin.

"This, you like this? Is it smooth? You like my skin, right? Touch it," she directed.

Jennifer smiled, even shook a little. She did what she was told to do and touched Regan.

Jennifer had felt her own private area, she had touched herself before. She knew how it felt. But this was different. Regan's lips were pink, kind of blushed, and smooth.

The women were leaning against the antique bed now, with Regan taking control. She held Jennifer's wrist now. With a tight grip, she moved Jennifer's hand against her skin.

"Touch me, just a little," Jennifer asked. Regan reached down between Jennifer's closed thighs.

"You like that, don't you?" Both women were becoming more playful.

"Yeah, I do. I like that," Jennifer answered, breathless.

Regan put her lips against Jen's mouth and kissed softly, seductively. She opened her mouth slightly. Then Regan lowered her body to meet Jen on the end of the bed. She knelt in front of her.

Jen's arms fell by her sides, resting on the mattress. She leaned back. Regan placed a hand on each knee and gently opened Jen's legs. She removed everything but her panties. It happened so quickly and easily. Then, Regan was pleased. She saw what she suspected, a shapely woman who had hidden herself under layers of insecurity. She was determined to make Jennifer feel sexy again.

And she was…Jennifer was sexy. Regan told her so.

"Jen, your body, you are so sexy and you don't even know it. Let me show you. Lay back. Relax." Regan's quiet confidence guided Jen.

"Oh my God, this is so insane. I have never done anything like this."

"Ssshhh, you're okay, Regan told her. "You want to try this. So do I. No one has to know."

Why have I never done this before? Regan thought. She knew it wasn't necessarily being with a woman that excited her, but it was the freshness of it, the unknown, and the control. It was a beautiful escape.

She kissed her some more, teased her, moved against her. Jennifer's moans were so sweet. She was actually quite feminine, and sounded like a content purring cat.

"I like your shirt." They laughed. "Nice bra too," Regan went on, letting her fingers wander down and into Jen's blouse. Jennifer knew what she was referring to. Her blouse was sheer. The built-in camisole covered most of her torso, but the bra straps kept sliding out. She wore black tonight, instead of nude. Had she worn nude, it would go unnoticed. Jennifer didn't say a word. She liked the fact that Regan commented on her bra, that she noticed. Jennifer liked how Regan's fingers felt as she unbuttoned her blouse, tugging on her nipples.

Jennifer sat up some. *Am I really doing this?* She looked around the room at the inn, at Regan, and at the bed. Everything felt so new to her.

"Pretty buttons." Regan reached across Jennifer's blouse, taking a button in her fingertips. "I've always liked pearls." The buttons were pearly with a shimmery glaze. Jennifer finished her wine. Regan moved in closer now. Button in one hand, more wine in the other, Regan leaned into Jen, even closer, pretty much on top of her.

She straddled. Jennifer was underneath her, almost helpless. Regan unbuttoned all of her blouse. She held open Jennifer's legs with her knees. She pushed her knee between Jennifer's legs, keeping them parted at the thighs. Jennifer began to move against her, riding her leg, begging her to grind on her harder and faster. She breathed fast, telling Regan to give her more.

But Regan slowed down. She stopped and then no one moved. Regan grabbed her glass and swallowed, handing it to Jennifer, motioning for her to set it onto the nightstand. Jennifer reached over and put it onto the coaster. She did as she was told.

Regan had dipped two fingers into the glass before she finished it. She brought her fingers to Jennifer's lips. A warm burn.

"Here, taste. It's sweet. Suck my fingers." And she did. Jennifer parted her mouth so Regan could run the wetness along her bottom lip. Drops fell, the liquid slid down her mouth. Regan's fingers stayed on Jennifer's parted lips. Regan took her other hand and felt for Jennifer's nipples. She found one, erect and aroused.

They were lying on their sides now. Without hesitating, Regan pushed her knee between Jennifer's legs again, harder now, forcing them to open wider. She lowered herself down to the bed, squeezing a nipple. She pinched kind of hard. Jennifer closed her eyes and gasped. Regan lowered her hand to finger Jen...

A voice called up from below. "Hey, ladies? You coming down or what?" Now footsteps. Regan stopped, pulled away, and stood up in a hurry. They were holding back gasps and giggles.

Neither of them really knew what they were doing, but the skin on skin connection felt natural. It was nice to share intimacy with someone who didn't have expectations.

"Coming," Regan and Jennifer said in stereo

"Shit," they whispered, still laughing.

"Be down in a sec." Jennifer held her hand over her mouth, half whispering. "Sshhh! He would die. There is no way he would believe this," Jennifer looked at Regan for reassurance.

"You know," Regan began, "maybe he'd like it? Have you thought of that? Maybe all your marriage needs, all you need, is to spice it up. Remember who you were, who you are. Do you know what I mean? Like, open yourself up more, to him, to yourself, to your own sensuality. You don't realize how sensual you can be, do you?" She took a chance. "Do you want to invite him up?"

"No," Jennifer answered quickly, "but I know what you're saying. I feel it. I felt it with you. I watched you, I watched how Leo watched you, how he watches you. I want him to watch me like that—to want me. I want to feel again. I want to feel free. No, I don't want him in here... this is for me. I'll remember this."

Regan smiled and understood. She was relieved, actually. She knew it was time to get real. To stop acting. She began to look around at the books and papers strewn out of the bed. She couldn't get a line out of her head about friendship and lonesome times and sharing wine. She felt an urge to recite it to Jen, to share it, if only she could remember it, or find it. Regan reached for a journal, opened it, and found what she was looking for. She read it to Jennifer as they began picking their clothes off of the floor.

"Remember you asked what I did today? Well, here's what I was thinking about. It kinda reminds me of this weekend. It's from a song I was playing on my iPod earlier. I heard the song a hundred times, but the lyrics hit me today so I wrote them down," Regan shared. "There's this one line about needing people to make the lonesome times better. And this other line about how we're all a part of everything, the past, the present, and the future. We seek freedom and we spread our wings. They remind me of you in this moment. Fly on, proud bird; it's something like that. Feels like some lonely part in us needed to meet. This weekend has really helped me."

"What were you reading?" Jennifer was somewhat confused, but also intrigued. "I've heard that. This is crazy. I'm in bed with a stranger and she's reading me poetry or something."

Regan answered her. "You won't believe me, but this was actually written by Lynyrd Skynyrd en route to the funeral for Ronnie Van Zant. I know it's totally random. I mean, here we are in intellectual classical land and I'm reading Lynyrd Skynyrd. You have to see the humor here."

"I think I get what you're saying," Jennifer said. "I like the idea of being free. I haven't felt so free in a while."

"Hey, ladies!" Leo called again. The women burst into laughter and finished getting dressed.

"We better get going." Regan straightened up. Then they headed down the stairs together. Leo was on the last stair. He looked up at Jennifer and they locked eyes. He smiled at her. Something was different. Good different.

Chapter Sixteen

The locals had cleared out. Regan took a spot on the couch near the fire. The poet sat by the fire on the loveseat. Leo invited Regan and the poet to come to the tavern to get some drinks. A few people he met from the happy hour would be there. Regan declined. Jack, standing with the group, also declined and said he planned to get to bed early and be on his way early Sunday morning.

"Well then, if we don't get to say goodbye, have a safe trip. Good meeting you," Leo said firmly. The men shook hands. Jennifer reached toward the poet and gave a polite hug.

"Yes, have a safe trip. Hope you have a good weekend," Regan said.

"That I did," the poet replied.

"Are you going to bed early too, Regan? Leaving early as well?" Leo asked loudly, almost rudely.

Regan answered, "No, not me. I'll be up for a bit. And I'm staying a couple more nights."

"There's a lot of snow coming," Leo said. "Maybe you'll get snowed in?"

"Yes, then Gerta and I will have a splendid time." They all laughed.

"There are snowshoes, I noticed," Leo pointed out. More laughter.

"Well, if I get snowed in, at least there's the tavern. Have a good time, you guys," Regan said, trying to redirect Leo.

"Yes, and I heard there's a book signing Sunday night. Not sure who, though, some of the locals were talking about it." Jennifer said she had overheard a conversation about the bookstore.

"All I know," interrupted Leo, "it's Saturday night and we have no kids and no deadlines. Let's go eat. And drink. And be merry."

"Sounds perfect," said the poet. "You two enjoy yourselves. Great meeting you all." Everyone smiled.

"Yes, you guys have a great dinner. Jennifer, thanks for the drink," Regan couldn't resist adding.

Both the women smiled. Jennifer held Leo's hand.

"Bye," Jennifer said. "Maybe we'll see you later?"

"Maybe," Regan said, but knew otherwise. She had zero interest or desire to see Leo again.

Leo sensed he had gotten as far as he was going to get—as far as she was going to let it—and he was okay with that, though he acted a tad rejected. He did what he could to shake it off.

He had Jennifer there, on his arm, and he felt her. Tonight, he felt her presence. He felt something again. How long it had been. He felt she was really there with him. So different than when they arrived. He was grateful.

He knew very little about Regan, this mystery woman from the inn, and only learned now that she was staying a few more days. What was her story? Whatever it was, he had a touch of gratitude for meeting her, almost compelled to thank her, but he resisted. He wasn't sure what he would thank her for, but he sensed a shift in himself. It confused him. Here was a stranger he met at an inn who had done something to him, to his wife, but he wasn't sure exactly what.

She seemed to reignite a fire he assumed went out long ago. He appreciated this woman, but who was she? Had they not met, he would not have known his marriage was on simmer with a dull flame—a pilot light that had not, in fact, burned out. Regan was the kindling; she turned up the heat.

He felt saved.

The couple left for dinner and everyone said heartfelt goodbyes. They all seemed genuinely glad to have this weekend at the magical inn out in the lovely, snowy Berkshires. Jack told Regan she missed quite a crowd while she and Jennifer were having girl talk.

He filled her in. For a bunch of townies gathered at the happy hour, this sure had been an intelligent bunch. Lots of musicians and artists and people with great stories. Many seemed to have literally stepped out of life—some from the city—who deliberately decided to get out of the rat race, slow down, and live a quiet life.

Regan began to tune out the poet. She got lost in her own thoughts. The peacefulness of the weekend began to take hold. She loved the area of Stockbridge and Lenox. How nice to have a happy hour at an inn. A wine tasting the night before. A great sushi meal in the middle of the country. A tavern in walking distance. And a book signing. Maybe she'd go. The town surprised Regan. She was impressed with the small paper, *The Berkshire Eagle*, that sat on the coffee table — it was known as the best local newspaper in the country.

It was quite a hidden gem out here. She wondered why she hadn't done something like this before. How wonderful it must be — how it is — to walk out of life.

She liked being in a place where no one knew her past. She could be anyone she wanted to be.

She wondered who the author was. She heard Gerta talking about this well-known man. She wondered when he was flying in. Would he make it in time or would the runways be iced over? Who would get snowed in with her? She hoped weather would get in his way. She wanted to be alone. She had her fun. Now she was ready for some peace and quiet. No new distractions.

She'd miss the cozy downstairs of the inn if the newcomer was overbearing — self-involved, ego-driven, boring, odd, obnoxious, nosey, loud, or well, fill in the blank. She worried too much.

I can always hide away in my room, she thought. Regan was always a step ahead, planning out even the smallest of details. She always had an escape route. And, contrary to her desire to find the best in people, she always assumed the worst. She grew tired of having her guard up all the time; what other way was there?

If I have to retreat to my room, it will be okay, she decided. Nothing, no one could be more interesting than the events and people from the past day and night.

She was in for a surprise.

The poet finished his monologue and Regan tuned back in. They said their pleasantries and parted ways; both had quiet plans of their own. They seemed to understand each other's need for space within the inn, and there was an unspoken code of respect. Jack didn't push Regan. He took her cue and went about his business.

This was the first day Regan remembered unplugging since losing Grace. She began to feel the inn's healing powers. The evening turned into night, and a feeling of contentedness settled into Regan's soul.

BETH JANNERY

Chapter Seventeen

It was nice to sit for a few minutes. The white linen or thick cotton couch sank when she sat. There were too many pillows to adjust. Regan took the time to settle into the softness, busily creating a nook. Even slouched into the comfort, Regan's posture was flawless. She tucked one of the smaller pillows behind her back, lowering her hips, rear, and thighs down into the cushions that looked bleached and sundrenched even in the dark of the evening. Years ago, Regan remembered hearing or reading or being told by her mother that the key to straight and upright shoulders was the small of the back. If the tail of the back was erect it automatically forced the upper torso into proper position. She knew these things; she paid attention.

After her mother died, Regan sat in a room of somber adults. There was a musty smell, an old smell that hung in the air. She fixated on back bumps and shoulder slumps. Necks protruded horizontally instead of vertically. She watched as people held drinks in one hand and dessert plates or crackers, cheese, and cocktail napkins in the other. They leaned over too much. She didn't like it and made a quiet promise to herself not to let that happen. Her mother had beautiful posture, not like the dank room of relatives and visitors who had come to pay their respects.

She wanted to believe her mother was perfect — not the selfish, Cancer-ridden alcoholic she actually was.

Her memory of this made Regan prop the bottom pillow up even more. Somewhere along the way, she made the connection that good posture set her apart from others. She liked nuggets of anything that kept her mother alive. She smiled at the memory and was glad she knew the secret. Too many women inhaled, threw their shoulders back, forcing their boobs to jut out. It looked fake.

She stretched her arms above her head and pointed her toes. How comfortable she was here. How the couch welcomed her. Regan lifted her legs and folded them under her body. She eyed the coffee table books, tempted to reach for the one about the Berkshire landscape, but she resisted. The moment called for nothing but stillness, a nice break in the commotion of the last two hours. Her eyes closed as she breathed in deeply through her nose — *one, two, three, four,* she counted silently and slowly, releasing her breath for four. Relaxing into the rhythm, she repeated the brief meditation, taking in the warm smell and crackling of the fire.

Regan felt a presence, even with her eyes shaded. She looked up, remembering the poet was nearby. When she sat down, he was in the far corner of the room scanning the many shelves. He left her deliberately to settle in and have a moment for herself before he approached her.

She wasn't bothered when she opened her eyes to see him again, standing at the end of the couch, book in hand.

"Hey there," he said.

"Hey." She smiled back. "Grab a seat if you want."

He removed two pillows, making room on the loveseat across the table. Jack noticed Regan looking at his hand. He held the book her way. "Mockingbird," he said. "*To Kill a Mockingbird*, cliché, but one of my favorites. It made me want to write."

The urge to roll her eyes was overwhelming, but she resisted. "That and all the classics," she said. "I bet everyone wants to write the great American novel."

"It's true," he agreed, "but few of us actually go into the field. Being in the literary field has drawbacks."

"Oh yeah? Like what? I don't even know what you actually do."

"Well, the paychecks, that's the biggest drawback."

This she knew was the common complaint of writers.

"They are few and far between, especially for poets."

"But worth it?"

"At times. Mostly, yes, if it is your first love."

"I get it," she said. "It's admirable. I'd love to see your work. Tell me one."

"What? Now? No way," he laughed. "No way in hell."

"Oh, okay, I see how it works. You're one of those?"

"That I am, but..." He paused. "But, I'm actually good, damn good." Jack's face lit up when he spoke of his passion for writing. "Nowadays, I write little poetry. It's more of a passion or hobby. I mostly do translations, or comparative lit projects. Blah, blah, blah."

Regan didn't really know what that meant — comparative literature projects? She had some sort of vague idea, but not enough interest to ask. She sat with a slight disappointment that Jack wouldn't recite a poem on command. She watched him. His eyes lowered and he laughed, shaking his head.

"Good for you," she said kindly. "I mean it. Too many people don't give themselves credit. I mean, you do what you love and you're good at it. What's better than that?" Even if he didn't get paid to write poetry for a living, she was impressed that he pursued his craft. It was rare to find someone who actually did what he loved for a living.

"Enough about me. Enough about work," he said playfully.

Regan sat still, continuing to watch him. He changed positions, adjusting himself. Then they both stopped and listened to the quiet in the room.

She observed he seemed somewhat uncomfortable, but she was unwilling to break the silence. He appeared to be okay with it. She found the quiet moment both amusing and tender. The other day, he was aggressive and rough. Now, he was almost awkward and boyishly goofy. He was truly charming, even if at first introduction his profession did force her to yawn. She scolded herself for not giving him the benefit of doubt the first night at dinner. Then again, the other night, she was a tad preoccupied, what with Leo's fingers slipped inside her panties.

Then, as if he was able to read her thought, he looked at her directly. "We're a lot alike, you and me."

"Really? What makes you say that?"

"You know, we both use our brains and we think. We think, probably too much, and we need to turn it off. I saw you disconnect. I watched you. The harder I pushed on your wrists, the further away you went." He began to go to a place that made Regan both uncomfortable and aroused.

110

She saw where he was going. Verbal foreplay. She wasn't sure she wanted to go there tonight. She made the decision to boldly put on the brakes.

"Right, I fuck like a man. And tonight, well, I'm not fucking anyone. So how about you open that book you've been flipping the pages of this whole time, and read something? If you aren't going to recite some of your poetry, at least you can give me a small chunk of a classic."

BETH JANNERY

Chapter Eighteen

Regan made him laugh. She was funny. He was drawn in.

"Look at who's directing now?" Jack said. "See, I told you we're similar." He didn't miss a beat, opening up to a page in *Mockingbird*, invisibly dog-eared as if he waiting to read it all evening.

He began reading to her.

"'They're certainly entitled to think that, and they're entitled to full respect for their opinions...but before I can live with other folks I've got to live with myself. The one thing that doesn't abide by majority rule is a person's conscience.'"

"That's Atticus," he said.

"Yeah, no kidding. I know Atticus." Regan rolled her eyes. And he caught her.

One passage from Harper Lee's novel and I'm fiercely uncomfortable. It's like this guy, this poet, this stranger saw right through me. This stranger I slept with before knowing his last name.

"What's your last name?" I interrupted.

"Wait your turn," he shot back.

I can't tell if he's joking, annoyed, or role playing. I could play with it, play with the sexual undertones, but I was pretty sure he'd be pissed I was interrupting. He was already continuing into the next passage. I could tell I was right; he didn't want to play.

"Atticus again," he said. I'm unsure if the poet was condescending or just helpful, instructional almost. So I dropped it and tried not to think the worst. Why did I always think the worst? *Note to self: work on that.*

I knew the *Mockingbird* excerpts, but saw no need to get into a pissing contest. It was a damn book, after all. Poet guy continues.

"'I wanted you to see what real courage is, instead of getting the idea that courage is a man with a gun in his hand. It's when you know you're licked before you begin but you begin anyway and you see it through no matter what. You rarely win, but sometimes you do.'"

He read on…

"'She seemed glad to see me when I appeared in the kitchen, and by watching her I began to think there was some skill involved in being a girl…'"

He stopped and looked at me. I was deliberately quiet. Wonder where this would go if I didn't say a word. So much is said in silence.

Now the silence was uncomfortable, but I swore I wouldn't break it. Poet turned to another section and began to read again.

"'What I meant was, if Atticus Finch drank until he was drunk he wouldn't be as hard as some men are at their best. There are just some kind of men who—who're so busy worrying about the next world they've never learned to live in this one, and you can look down the street and see the results.'"

"That was Miss Maudie," he pointed out.

At this point, it didn't matter what *To Kill a Mockingbird* was about. I was more focused on the passages he'd selected. There seemed to be meaning behind all of them. I wanted to know why he selected them. But I knew he wanted me to ask. I didn't like giving people what they wanted anymore. I didn't like giving people what they were waiting to see. I should play along, perhaps, but it was more fun this way.

Then another thought came. The idea appeared to watch and wait and wonder. And to see how long until he kissed me again.

Game on.

Chapter Nineteen

Now the fun begins, I think. It'll go either of two ways. One way is for me to be coy and listen and let him direct and teach, and I'll go with the flow.... The only other way I see it is if we get all uber intellectual and literary and really fuck. Not much sexier than a well-read man.

But then began the next passage.

And I never saw it coming.

Jack stood up and straightened his trousers. I liked the wide whale cords—neatly pressed with just enough wear to look disheveled. His hands press down on his quads, moving the brown, thick fabric downward.

Then he sat closer to me with his knees staring directly at mine. If I wasn't careful with how I'd positioned my long legs, he would be aiming his muscle right between my legs. Fully clothed, I felt vulnerable. Any myth of control, on my part, had been shattered. He leaned into me and read.

A warm bolt of unease shot into my gut. I had to force myself to think, to pay attention. Something new was happening. I was careful now, didn't want to interrupt him.

Then, right before he began reading, he looked at me.

"How are you doing?" I think he asked how I was doing, but essentially heard nothing. "You ready for more, Regan?" His question sounded more like a demand. "Regan, pay attention." His face illuminated in a soft, warm smile. I returned the smile. "Okay," he continued, "this next part is Scout. It's the last part I'll read. *'Neighbors bring food with death and flowers with sickness and little things in between. Boo was our neighbor. He gave us two soap dolls, a broken watch and chain, a pair of good-luck pennies, and our lives. But neighbors give in return. We never put back into the tree what we took out of it: we had given him nothing, and it made me sad.'* What? Tell me your reaction. Where are you right now?" He placed the open book across one knee and breathed down my neck. He was directly across from me, but I felt him invading my space.

Why is he probing? I began to worry.

"I don't know what to say," I stammered. "What do you want me to say?" I always knew what to say.

Where was this coming from? My mind was racing.

"Why are you digging?" I began to close off. "I feel like you're digging, like you know something." I folded my arms. I wondered, *What now? We're supposed to talk about the passage? Analyze? I'm not doing this.*

"Regan, do you like being a mystery?"

I acted like I had no clue what he was talking about. "A mystery? What are you talking about?"

This is not why I'm here. I don't want to sit on the couch with you and talk about fucking funerals and death and sickness. I bit my lip and just listened, trying to laugh it off, blame it on too much wine. Too much too fast after all the B&B. I was still buzzed from my rendezvous with Jen, but the high is beginning to fade, making me somewhat lucid.

"You like fast." He looked right at me. "You like too much. Don't you. Regan? Don't you?"

I was a million miles away. It must be the wine.

I excused myself and went into the restroom off of the living room. He'd managed to undress me, again, even if only verbally this time.

I splashed water on my face. The room I'd entered was slow motion. It was as if the world had stopped and all I could feel were the drips of water building on my chin. The time it took one to fall into the white porcelain sink, which needed to be cleaned, I imagined Jen and Leo were toasting down the hill at the restaurant. And the other guests or townies were biting into their appetizers by now. I wanted to run.

Drying my hands, patting my cheeks, faking a flush. It took only moments, but it was an eternity. Honesty. I decided honesty was the only way for me, tonight, to walk out of this tiny bathroom and speak the truth. And there I went. It was that, or I hide in my room.

He was still on the couch, but the book was closed now. I started to tell the poet that family, past, death, funerals, it all had to be off limits. I didn't want to go there. Not tonight.

"Regan, I get it." He stood up, walked closer. "Sshh, come here. Don't say a word."

I got a warm hug. Gentle and protective. He knew exactly what he was doing.

"Listen, let's forget it all. I get you. There is this past. Let's leave it alone. I won't ask another question," he promised. "Here's what we are going to do," he continued with quiet confidence. He handed me a room key. His room key. I knew it was his. The metal was warm. The number was on it and he directed me upstairs. This was not what I had been planning. But now I didn't want to think.

He knew how to make me escape.

"Let me help you forget." Jack looked directly into me.

"You have no idea," I responded.

"No, I don't know the details, but I know. I know you are alone, and it's okay. I know you have always felt alone. I know that is the way you want the world to see it. But tonight, you're not going to be alone. You are going to be mine. I am going to make you mine."

He pushed the key into my hand and told me he was going to make me forget everything.

"Go, go upstairs."

"Okay," I answer. "Now?"

"Yes, now." His voice was more playful. "Yeah, get your sexy ass upstairs and wait for me."

The laughing felt good.

"All those walls, Regan. Someday, someone is going to find you and tear them all down."

"Nah, I won't let them." I turned and smiled back.

"Well, if he asked, you'd never let him stay. But someone will find you and he'll walk right in and take over and you won't know what hit you. He'll take away all your armor. He'll take care of you. "

She heard his words trail off as she turned the upstairs corner and he disappeared into the inn's pantry.

Take care of me? It had been too long.

When had anyone taken care of her? Years, if ever. Tonight wasn't the night to think about it.

So much for a quiet night in her room with a good book. She thought she had finished with the poet the other afternoon. Then finished with Leo. And Jen, finished off

Jen. Now, the poet was back for more. What a weekend. What the hell was she doing? Didn't matter much since everyone was checking out in the morning.

Tomorrow, she'd be back to normal.

The key worked on the first try and she made herself at home, just as Jack suggested.

Regan remembered his instructions. Dim the lights. Put on something comfortable. Wait for him under the covers.

She liked doing as she was told. She didn't have to think. As she slipped into her bare feet, bra, and panties, she heard glasses clank and the fridge door close. He wasn't far behind.

A classic white oxford lay at the foot of Jack's bed next to a plaid throw that looked too scratchy to snuggle in. She chose the men's shirt and contemplated taking the bra and panties off. Or should she leave them on? Ah, decisions and a cloudy wine brain. It would have been embarrassing if he walked in. For starters, she was talking to herself about the pros and cons of undergarment wear. Secondly, she was worrying he might think she was being too promiscuous. Taking her panties off might suggest she was — is rather — planning to get laid.

How funny. It was like the Thursday nights in college. Go to the frat party with sexy panties, and the boy you hook up with thinks you're a slut. On the other hand, wear boy briefs and forget to trim your bikini line and you'll be less likely to mess around. The silly games girls played. Why bother? Regan made a vow right then and there to always be bare and always wear her favorite lacy thongs. Not for him. Not for any man. Not for what he might or might not think. But because she liked the feel of her soft skin, and because she liked the cling and tug of a well-fitted thong.

This was one of the first decisions she made for herself, because it was something she liked and she wanted. The weekend at the inn already had positive changes. She was glad she came. The expression "throwing caution to the wind" came to mind. She mouthed the word "promiscuous," and started laughing.

What a stupid word. It was one word, something one of her friend's moms had used once. Her teenage friends were doing what they thought was normal exploration. Hormones were raging. The girls were experimenting with makeup and miniskirts, talking about the game results of Spin the Bottle, which the mom overheard. Nothing more than the other girls and boys, or so she thought. That one word, promiscuous, at the lips of her friend's mother.

"Girls, you must learn to play your cards close to your vest," she spoke in a condescending tone. "You wouldn't want to be thought of as promiscuous." Regan didn't even know what the mom meant, but she nodded in order to continue to be liked.

Ouch. How deep wounds could cut. It still made her cringe. From now on, that word was going to mean something positive, something powerful. *It is a choice I'm making, and I'm empowered. I want to be promiscuous.* Regan wasn't sure if she was thinking these thoughts or saying them aloud. *I want to witness my body reacting to a man's touch.*

There was something liberating in that moment.

No apologies for being a sexual being.

Her thoughts quieted as the poet approached her. Now she was all his, at least for the next hour.

She was already planning her exit.

Chapter Twenty

"You saw *9 ½ Weeks*, right?" Jack asked as he opened the door.

He was in the room now. "What kind of question is that?" Regan answered.

The anticipation grew ten-fold the last three minutes. Once Regan got herself set up, positioned her body under the covers just like he said to do, all that was left was the wait. Now, he was right there with her, in the dark, walking closer to his bed.

She liked being under his sheets. Since she'd felt him inside her just two showers ago, she made herself wet again by the mere thought of him penetrating her, which she knew would happen in a few moments.

"This is much better than reading literary passages," she laughed.

"Ah, don't discount the foreplay," he said without missing a beat. "Your eyes are closed, just like I told you?" Jack checked on the instructions he'd given to Regan.

"Yes, they're closed." She had a nervous giggle now.

"Good girl. You're a very good girl. I'm going to find out what's under those covers," he said as he approaches her. She could sense him coming closer.

Regan tried to sit up. She could feel his heaviness in the air. She couldn't see a thing, not even an outline. She did what she was told and kept her eyes locked. She sensed he was standing over her, over the bed. She felt his hand reach for her. He was next to the bed just as she thought. He stroked her hair, gently, hushing her, directing her not to speak. He found her mouth. She waited.

"Put this on." He held two fisted hands near her face. She shifted, allowing the poet full access to her face, hair, and neck. He was blindfolding her. Not that she could see anyhow, but the thought that a thick, sash was tightening around her eyes and head was invigorating.

"You've done this before?" She could tell he had.

The attention of detail he was paying to her shouldn't be mistaken as special. She knew he must be a master at getting women to do what they wanted for him. By asking the question, she'd taken some control back, let him know that she knew he was a player, and she let on that she was not foolish enough to think this was just for her. She felt in control for the simple reason that she didn't care if she ever saw the poet again. She was utterly in the moment.

He knew her thoughts. Before she could finish, he stopped her. "Ssshhh, I told you to stop talking. This is just for you. I only want you. Right here, right now, you are going to be all mine. Here's how it works, Regan. It's just the two of us." As he talked to her he began to trace her neckline. "It's the two of us," he continued. "There is no one else. No past, no future. No memories. No expectations. Just right here, right now. Be here with me.

Can you do that, Regan?" His voice was so tender. "Let me help you forget everything."

The attention made Regan shudder. She couldn't recall the last time a man pursued her like this. It was the best drug she could imagine. She worried the letdown would be as intense as the high.

He had no idea what a task it was to get her to forget. He said he could help her forget everything. He had no clue what a tall order that was. It was exactly what she wanted, what she needed.

She stopped fighting him, and slowly began to unwind; his fingers checked the knot around her head. The blindfold was tight, almost too tight. And now, his fingertips swirled around her collarbone and shoulder tip, and the tracing began to lower down to her cleavage. It was a perfectly peaceful moment. Regan was spread out under his covers, in his white dress shirt with black panties and bra, and a sash across her face. He was sitting down by her side now, the blanket lowered, uncovering her chest. His hand lowered it some more. Then he stopped.

"What do I do? What do you want me to do? I feel like I'm just laying here." Regan had no idea how to stop and be still. "It's so uncomfortable," she confessed.

His voice rose. "I told you to stop talking. Get comfortable with it. Stay still. Don't move." Jack lit a candle next to the bed and held it over her. One drip of wax, of hot wax, fell between her breasts. Then another one.

Regan gasped, then slowly inhaled. She listened to his voice telling her not to move. "Don't make a sound. There's more. One more. Here it comes."

Drip. And another. Drip. One more. Then he stopped abruptly.

"More," she said. "I want more."

The room was so quiet she thought she could hear the single candle flame. He withheld the hot wax from her skin.

She heard herself, her voice almost unrecognizable. "I want more." He thought she was talking about the heated wax, and she was, in part.

But she also wanted more—of life. She wanted so much more.

This was a problem. Regan had her feet in both worlds. She wanted to distract and explore and enjoy. She wanted to let go and let the rush of him flow over her. But she knew it wasn't real. She didn't feel anything for this man. She liked being with Jen, but she hadn't felt anything. She liked Leo's attention, but she didn't like Leo. She had no interest in another woman's husband. No interest in a woman. No interest in being a woman who enticed married men. That wasn't her. No interest in the man whose bed she had slipped into. No interest in seeing Jack again. She needed no one. She told herself this again and again.

She had no interest in anything but forgetting her daughter's death. But nothing stopped it for more than a moment. The hot wax was a temporary fix, a Band-Aid on her open wound. Nothing made the hurt go away.

Not the hot wax that burned her skin temporarily. Not the pain or pleasure sensation. Not the brandy. Not the wine. Not the cold ice he was melting on her heat. Nothing. No one. She was distracted, but she was still there. She was utterly lost. But she was still there.

The sounds from the hallway jolted her. Leo and Jen were back. Their footsteps were heavy. Her body was light. She was floating.

Regan was lying in his bed. Her blindfold had come off. She stayed still in the bed, but she was watching the hallway. She was wandering through a childhood field, and she was strapping in the car seat in the back. She was changing the song on her iPod, she was texting, she was putting the lid on the hot coffee and she was thinking of the lyrics, from "Falling Awake," and that's just the way it goes…

The ice wasn't cold or hard any longer. Now it was melted and wet, almost annoying, like a spill. She thought it needed to be wiped up. He shoved a finger into her. He was still there and she was already gone. How could two people be so far apart? Regan had lost interest.

She'd felt farther apart than this with Noah. At least the poet was tangible. She could feel his desire. With Noah, he was always gone. She could go through the motions or she could give him her everything, and it was always the same. He would mount her, ride her, and come inside her. Maybe he'd satisfy her, but it would take her mental energy and fantasy to reach climax with Noah. She'd always leave, in her mind, and he'd come. And then he'd be gone. If it wasn't on a business trip, it would be on his laptop or smart phone. She knew it was over years before it was over. Why was it hitting her so hard tonight?

This trip is painful. Regan scolded herself for thinking too much.

She was lost in her memories and she was lost from the moment. She didn't want to be in either place. She had to get out of there.

She stood on the cliff, about to fall backwards. She felt his fingers penetrate her again.

"Stop." Regan was abrupt about it. She didn't care. She was done. She had to get out of there. She had to flee.

There was nowhere she had to be, no other place she had to get to. Just not here. She got up, was as honest as she could be, knocked over the cup of ice cubes, which had turned to liquid, and she spilled it all on the wood floor.

It was messy. She was messy. Nothing was tidy. She needed to get clean.

It was in that moment that Regan knew she was broken and alone. They said a breakdown, a rock bottom, could be a spiritual awakening. There was nothing spiritual about this moment other than the hurt and pain.

She had never felt so empty, but she wasn't in a place where she could cry out, not yet. She needed the dark. She needed her room. She needed to lock the door and hide away and pull the covers over her head. She knew the time had come to stop. She needed to stop.

Stop.

And in this stopping, came the freedom.

In the freedom, came the awakening.

For the moment, for right now, it would be enough to get out of the arms of the strangers and into a place of her own.

She didn't want anyone if she couldn't have Grace.

She wanted Grace. She needed Grace. She only needed Grace.

Grace.

Grace was gone.

Chapter Twenty-one

Being single again was a funny thing. She knew all the rules, and knew she would most likely break them too. It was just like a woman to be needy, to be too into a man, to get physical too fast and then wonder, gee, where did he go? If you actually liked the guy then you didn't sleep with him too quickly. The mistake was always made—an emotional, intimate bond was not connected or created during sex. Contrary to how it made a woman feel, sex was sex. It was fucking.

There was nothing emotional about it. So don't get the two mixed up—intimacy and sex were two different worlds. If you fucked too soon, then you'd only have that world. If you wanted a shot at an emotional connection, be a friend. Period. No way around it. Fuck too soon and he was gone and there you were, wondering what the hell just happened, again. If women could only get this, really get this, then the two worlds would not collide.

She made the mental note—*when you think you could actually like the guy, be friends. Be patient. When you want to have fun, just fuck him and walk away. Perfect.* She knew the rules of life. The women that mixed up the two worlds

131

lived in a state of hurt and confusion. The idea that if you didn't hear from him and he didn't call and he makes no time for you then, as a clever book title said, he's not that into you. Period. Anything else was smoke and mirrors. If a guy liked you, he'd make time for you. Friends made time for friends. Lovers made time for more.

This was what Regan learned as a married woman; she watched all the mistakes single women made. Right now, she vowed not to make the same mistake as so many who went before her. She'd be fine being alone. She'd make up her own rules.

Chapter Twenty-two

She settled a lot in her marriage. She often felt something deep in her gut, but dismissed it and did what was expected. The unexpected part about being single again was finding out who she was in reaction, in response to others. She liked feeling how her body reacted to the new men, and one woman, who walked into her life this weekend.

This weekend at the inn would mark her in ways she did not yet know. She knew the life she lived. She watched the lives of others around her, and she learned from them—she knew how not to be by watching the single girl mistakes women made. She felt grateful for these lessons.

She knew where she came from. Sort of knew where she was going. But right now, she was in this spot where she had to reconcile the past. Wasn't she enough for him? She would never doubt herself again.

But first, she had to go through the pain. Pain was such a great agent for change. It was the ultimate equalizer. She wanted to change. She didn't want to be second best to anything or anyone again. She needed to come to terms with Noah. It wasn't the marriage she wanted. She wasn't the best person she could be.

She wouldn't settle again.

There were times when she and Noah laughed uncontrollably. Usually one or both of them were drinking. Nothing to excess, but it was used in a way to either dull the pain or enhance the fun. It was a way to alter her mood. They'd have fun, go out, meet with friends, hit a few "who's who" parties, and then make love after a few glasses and after paying the sitter, and then crash. They enjoyed each other and they were good company for a time, at least Regan thought so. But their intimacy never cracked the surface. Sure, they'd get physical and enjoy role plays or dive into some sort of sexual fantasy. But there wasn't the deep core intimacy that Regan craved. And she thought Noah simply didn't need it. She wanted Noah to really see her, to look into her, to penetrate her emotional layers. Noah was fine on the surface. If anything deeper existed, he wasn't aware of it or he lacked the desire to discover it.

Before she pulled away and lost herself in raising Grace, she agreed to a few lifestyle parties. And he'd often bring up the idea of inviting in another partner. If she wanted to have an affair with a sexy woman, he wouldn't have been bothered by that. Certainly this must be the sign of modern strength.

Or he'd talk about what aroused him; he wanted to watch her being fucked by another man. He wanted to swing. He may stray and explore and experiment, but it wasn't cheating because he always invited her along. He wanted her to be close to him. Or so she convinced herself. What kind of warped love was that? She knew right from wrong, but Noah had a way of convincing her that he was hers and she was his and anything extramarital was purely physical. But she always felt the divide. Regan stopped being able to distinguish between what was right and wrong, she lost her moral code for living, and took on his. She wanted the two to coincide—being physical and intimate went hand in hand. At least this was her shaky definition. She was learning at the inn that physical love has nothing to do with intimacy.

While this marriage or arrangement may have worked for some, it left Regan feeling empty. It only happened once in a while early in the marriage, but the betrayals left deep scars. She felt he never knew her.

Turning away from Noah and toward her fierce desire to mother and protect Grace was a gradual process. She did not decide one day to avoid intimacy. Regan knew in her heart that something was off. This was not how she wanted to be loved. So she set out to love Grace the way a daughter deserved to be loved—the way anyone would want to be loved.

She took everything she had and gave it to Grace. She reached inside and pulled out everything she needed as a daughter herself that she never received from a selfish and then ill and then dead mother, and she turned it into love for Grace. It was creating reality from fantasy, although Regan didn't know the difference at the time. All she knew was an emptiness, and she wanted Grace to always be filled up with love. So she did her best, really, as any mother would.

Noah retreated in the opposite direction. Although he adored Grace, his affection began to wander. He worked later than usual, he complained about the pressures of fatherhood combined with home duties and the workplace. Too much was expected of him. When they weren't fighting, they were alone. It was very rare to be in a room of three. Noah would disappear early in the morning and go to work. Travel increased and there was no such thing as the family dinner table. When he would make an appearance, Regan was so full of resentment, she'd retreat. It slowly eroded to a lonely marriage, masked and hidden behind a beautiful home and white picket fence.

Regan was alone often. This was her theme. A familiar pattern. She got used to it and she felt terrible for not appreciating how hard Noah was working. She was lucky to stay home, but she rarely voiced this appreciation to her husband. And when the clues about his affair became impossible to ignore, Regan did what any housewife in denial would do. She ignored them. Brushed them aside. Dove into her motherly duties. Catered to Grace and separated herself from her husband.

She fragmented as she had as a girl when her mother died; it was easy to do when Noah wasn't around. Although he didn't "leave her," in her mind, he left her. It was subtle abandonment. It stung. The marriage was killing her. She would die a slow death. And then she witnessed his betrayal.

Chapter Twenty-three

Regan woke up from a sound slumber realizing it was already Sunday morning. She felt a world away from when she started driving west on the Mass Pike. She rolled the weekend at the inn around in her head. She laid in bed and replayed her arrival on Friday—her afternoon nap, the wine tasting at the inn, dinner with strangers, her encounter with Leo, her tryst with Jen, her rendezvous—both—with the poet. Her head was spinning. She was thankful she left Jack's room when she did, grateful not to see any of the weekend guests again. All the goodbyes had been said.

She was craving some alone time and ran through the twists and turns of the weekend. All good, she decided. She smiled instead of regret.

Still, she wasn't sure who she was right now—a blur of confusion and loss and sensuality all rolled into one.

Regan wouldn't have changed a single moment from the weekend at the inn, but she was tired, emotionally spent. She was ready for people to check out. The time had come; nothing like this weekend escape could exist for very long. She knew she needed to focus on the past few months, have some quiet time, and begin to heal.

Today, she would go to Kripalu, the local wellness and meditation retreat center located in the Berkshires. Then maybe she would check out the bookstore and have a quiet dinner or read in her room. She liked plans. They framed her days. Maybe one day, she would have a life framework, but not yet. That was too much to think about. If she planned past today, well, past the next couple of months of being in the Berkshires, she would get too overwhelmed. Regan had no idea where she was headed or what was next; she could barely breathe in the day in front of her let alone plan the next chapter.

Slow down, she whispered, *see what comes*. She was open to anything that came. She was exhausted from living. She was willing to try something new. She wondered if it was true what she'd been told — be still and let life wash over you. She wondered if she did this what the tides would pull up.

She started to think past the day — the logistics swarmed her busy beehive. She went through the checklist of staying Sunday night and nothing but rest on Monday. Staying Monday night and checking out Tuesday. She would meet the realtor, who would give her the house keys for the year's rental. Regan imagined a woman with blonde sculpted hair, well-preserved, and perfect lipstick. Lip liner even, like her mother. Her mother had been a realtor. She played the role well. A drunk. Mumblings of a story she had heard about her mom being the best realtor in town — did a lot of coke and gave the rich builder in town blow jobs so she'd get the contracts. Regan worked hard to be nothing like her. She pushed the gossip aside and attempted to make the good of her mother remain.

There, her next few days were planned. Done. Check. Her year was sketched. At least now she had a rough outline. She was thankful for the opportunity to run a small safe house for teens out in the quiet country. The state had funded The Sojourn House for at-risk youth. Regan thought this was a fancy way of saying a runaway shelter. Her new job started in a week. She was already in love with the peaceful area where no one knew her past.

The Berkshires weren't so small these days; the area was more like intellectual country. People knew about the area and almost anyone she knew from New York had come out for a getaway.

It was an easy decision. Regan would take on the role for a year, maintain her privacy, and figure out what to do with the rest of her life. She didn't want to get to know anyone, wasn't planning to dive too deeply into work, and just sort of hoped to disappear from reality for a while. She had agreed to take the position for a year, and she was told that funding for future years wouldn't be difficult because people out in these parts liked supporting causes. But Regan wasn't thinking past a year.

She rented an old farmhouse for a modest amount each month, but hadn't even signed a formal lease. It was more of an email agreement from the owner she connected with through Craigslist.

"Charming old farmhouse available to one lucky renter. If you like cottage-style, old clapboard homes, you'll love this beauty. White-washed walls, open beams, raised ceilings, wide planked hard-wood floors beaten with love. Reply for pictures." This was a no-brainer for Regan. It had to be hers. The pictures showed an overgrown English-garden protecting the windy walkway filled with small grayish, slate-colored, and white stones. She was sold.

Within twenty minutes of emails, the farmhouse became hers. The landlord didn't live in town and would mail the key to a local realtor who'd help with property maintenance issues if there were any. Regan was also told the owner could be easily convinced to sell, but wasn't quite there yet, which worked just fine for Regan because the thought of committing to anything scared her.

It had been a while since she worked full-time, so she was thankful her past social work experience and degrees carried her far. She felt excited and nervous. Life without Noah and Grace was unknown. A year in the Berkshires to sort things through was a good place to be. The plan was in place. It made sense.

She eased into the morning, stretching like a cat. The thought of the snow made her smile. The town would be quiet. The inn would be still. Most likely, the new guest wouldn't make it and the book signing would be postponed. Good, she thought. No small talk. No bullshit.

It was time to get up, finally, and make her way out for a walk—or trudge in the snow—and head over to Kripalu. Regan slipped into some dirty workout clothes she had thrown over the chaise at the foot of the bed. She knew the house would be quiet and needed her morning coffee. The aroma seemed to be coming out of the wallpaper. She headed downstairs and was greeted by a music stand at the foot of the stairs between the hallway and the breakfast room. A stenciled sign read: Today's Poem. She stood quietly and read an excerpt by Frost. The calligraphy, she guessed, was done by Gerta.

Regan grabbed her coffee and the local paper and headed back to her room for a few more moments of solitude. She didn't want to be there during checkout and she heard the rumblings of suitcase zippers and shuffling footsteps. Now she heard more voices talking about the storm that was coming. Regan was relieved that her new friends would get out in time, and was happy in her assumption that no new guests would arrive. The roads sounded bad. Fortunately, the shuttle for Kripalu was used to New England roads and was 4-wheel-drive, so she wouldn't be stuck. Sounded like the airports would shut down by mid-day. Goodbyes were overheard. Trunks were closed. Car doors shut. Engines started. She was alone at last.

Regan set her mug down and made her way out. She bundled up in a hat, mittens, a scarf, and huge boots. She resembled an awkward second grader going out to sled. There was an engine running in the driveway, wheels spinning. She assumed the plow had come to stay a step ahead of the snow fall. Just as she reached for the door knob, the front door opened, almost hitting her in the face.

"Hey, watch out," she snapped.

"Oh, so sorry, didn't see you," a man responded.

"Shit, you're here?" Regan said rudely to the stranger.

"Excuse me?" The stranger was confused.

"I mean, what I mean is, uh, I didn't think any more guests were coming," Regan stammered, trying to explain her rudeness.

"Well, I'm here. Sorry to disappoint," the man said.

"But the airports, aren't they closed?" Regan inquired.

"I came early. I drove. Who are—"

Before the man could finish is sentence, Regan walked past the new guest. She exhaled loudly, her morning obviously interrupted, and she abruptly left, closing the door behind her with one tug of the knob.

"Who are you?" He finished his thought. "Nice to meet you too," he said sarcastically under his breath, shaking his head.

Chapter Twenty-four

That must be him. Looked just like he did on his book jackets. Handsome. Disarming. Regan had heard he might be the guest, but she hadn't expected to be caught so off guard.

Regan walked, realizing how rude she had been. She didn't care. She resented the intrusion.

Samuel Kellogg was staying at the same inn. Great. She rolled her eyes.

So much for her plan to avoid people today. She made a mental note to continue about her day. Do her own thing.

She knew enough to brush off her rudeness with a brief apology later if she bumped into him at the inn. "Sorry, hadn't had my morning coffee." Something like that would suffice. Or, "Don't like snow. Not a morning person." None of which was true. With a brief and full smile, he'd quickly forgive her. "No worries," he'd say.

She pushed the encounter out of her mind and walked on. The leaves were the loveliest, she thought, when the snow was fresh and white. Like paint splatters. As her hour in the snow ticked on, there was a heavy dusting—the snow moved quickly. Reminded her of the flour sifter she'd see her grandmother use in the kitchen. Did women even use flour sifters anymore? The piece of tin would rust and get stuck, but her grandmother used it nonetheless. She had such a certain way about her. Such grace. Regan named Grace after her grandmother.

More walking, she was quiet and deep in thought, only sounds were her trudging along, her footsteps, her breath. Regan lost track of time. The drifts were getting heavy now. Great for snowballs. She was suddenly overcome with a desire to play. She stopped at the slight incline at the foot of the inn, fell back, and started flapping her arms and legs.

The new guest caught a glimpse of the mystery snow angel from his front window. It warmed his heart, brought his serious jaw to a smile.

She stopped, simply lay there, and let the snow fall. It touched her face. Her skin was cold, her fingertips were numb. She didn't move.

Regan reached back into her memory. When was the last snow angel Grace made? She couldn't recall. She wished she had paid more attention.

Suddenly, a sensation of maple syrup topped over snowballs came to mind. She could taste it. It was a sweet recollection.

Oh, Grace.

Oh, Grace.

Her wet mittens covered her eyes, adding to her new tears.

He was still watching her.

Regan arched her head back, knowing she was not so alone anymore.

She viewed the window, but upside down, it was hard to make out the figure past the panes.

Quickly, she straightened up and pulled herself together. She walked to the porch swing only a few feet up. Sat down. Looked around. Wiped her dripping nose into her sweater cuff, which had been hanging out the entire walk. It had frozen gunk on it. That made her laugh.

Then the man's image came to mind again. Regan wondered if he was watching her. And if so, for how long? In that unknowing moment, she'd let a stranger in. She was petrified at the thought of this stranger, the world-renowned Samuel Kellogg, seeing her cry. *What a mess he'll think I am. Rude and nasty and now teary.*

What did she even know about him?

Why did she care?

She thought about it. She knew enough. She saw what everyone else saw, before he left his public life to live a quieter, private life. She knew he had a new book out and he must be feeding the beast in order to get book sales. She knew of his public image; it was a good one, and he helped many. But she also knew he made a concrete decision to avoid the press and live simply. She assumed he was in the Berkshires to promote his work. Maybe a New England tour, then heading to the west coast. He did something with big business, some sort of consulting or executive leadership.

He could easily have become a Tony Robbins type of figure, but he had a more serious, substantive aspect to his work. He seemed to appear in the press only when necessary and had a solid reputation. Still, she assumed he was wealthy, arrogant, and thought of himself to be somewhat of a celebrity. No doubt he'd be demanding on

Gerta and find the Berkshire towns to be small and too country to his liking.

Regan stopped herself. She always did this. She believed assumptions without facts. Just because a man came across as private did not mean he had a sense of entitlement or egotism. A quiet presence was often mistaken as arrogance. Odds were against anyone who came into contact with Regan without first proving themselves.

She wondered why he would stay at an inn. Certainly, he seemed like a Four Seasons kind of guy.

He could be almost ten years older, maybe early fifties or late forties. She'd guess a decade. Regan remembered hearing about a family tragedy he did not speak of. He was not one to wear his emotions or heart on his sleeve. Somehow, he had earned the reputation as a man's man. Men in big business or sports seemed to look up to him or easily identify with him. They looked to him and hired him for huge consulting fees to be their coach or mentor. She wasn't sure of the word.

Regan got up from the porch swing. The snow was blowing in all directions now; her rear was cold and wet. She shook off the chill and made the decision to set her thoughts of Samuel Kellogg aside, although she felt an undercurrent of excitement with him being at the inn; the snowstorm added to this. They were the only guests. Samuel, Regan, and Gerta.

She refocused. She felt ready to unplug. Kripalu awaited her arrival.

Chapter Twenty-five

The shuttle run to Kripalu was easier than expected. The 4x4 deftly traversed the slippery terrain. It was a straight shot, except for the narrowing of the road at the approach of the destination. A final climb gave a slight delay, but nothing the seasoned driver couldn't handle.

I was remembering a morning after the funeral when everything was settling down. I had things in place. I was beginning to sleep again. I was setting my plan in motion for this upcoming year. The plants had been watered. The beds had been made. Laundry was done. I was dotting my I's and crossing my T's and meeting a girlfriend for a walk. I didn't want to go. I wanted to be left alone, but I knew enough to get out of the house and check in with a couple of concerned acquaintances. I'd check in so they didn't appear at my door.

Hated that.

So, this particular morning, the morning after the funeral, I was almost handling life well and I was only two minutes away from heading out the door. I walked to the kitchen to drop a mug in the sink; the dishwasher was already going and this was the last dish. It slipped from my hand, crashing down onto the kitchen floor, drenching the kitchen area rug and staining it a dark brown.

This was my breaking point. This was my one-more-thing-that-couldn't-go-wrong. And then it did.

How I could get so pissed off at a spilled cup of coffee surprised me.

I was done. Spent. I couldn't handle anything else. I had nothing left.

I was afraid.

Then memories flooded in, washing over me as I was helpless on all fours, cleaning up the coffee.

An image of Grace sitting in her high chair came. I collected myself and made a point not to get angry at Grace.

"Oh, honey, it's just spilled milk," I would say. "It's okay, Lovey. It's okay, Lovey Lou. Accidents happen." I said this in a squeaky, high-pitched voice. The kind of voice dogs respond to. "Accidents happen."

Grace watched me wipe up the milk. I hoped she remembered me like this. I was careful not to overreact.

In that moment, I vowed not to resent Grace, not the way my mother resented me. I took an oath to do everything right. Didn't want her wasting money on years of therapy only to blame her mother.

Then, more memories. My memories. Of my mom.

"Do you know what I could have been?" she would say. "If I hadn't gotten pregnant, if didn't have a child? Do you have any idea? Do you? Do you? I sacrificed everything for you. I gave up everything."

Why is she telling this to me? I always wondered.

"You are so ungrateful," she said, screaming louder. "Do you have any idea?"

I did.

I heard the drunken tales every time she poured in at least three double gin martinis.

Her sacrifices. What she had to give up. The glamorous life. The life she longed for. How I had ruined her plans. I had it memorized.

She was made for much more than wiping spilled milk. She told me so. Many times.

Back in the kitchen with Grace, I vowed to gratefully wipe the milk up with a smile. She made me less selfish. I knowingly broke the cycle. Grace was watching. I was very careful not to let her see me angry. I would do anything for my Grace. I wanted her to remember me as carefree and laid back.

"Lovey Lou, don't cry over spilled milk."

"Sweet, sweet Grace," I often sang to her to the tune of "Sweet Jane," just replacing a few words here and there. Back at Kripalu I caught myself rocking slightly and my lips were moving to "Sweet Jane." I stopped immediately, careful no one saw me singing and swaying to myself.

BETH JANNERY

Chapter Twenty-six

Within minutes, I was checked in and had a moment to absorb my itinerary—morning prayer and meditation, yoga, a silent walk, a vegan lunch, then a small group session and a wrap-up guided meditation or a drum circle. My choice. I was not planning to choose the drum circle.

Everything was optional. I could stay half a day and blend in comfortably with the clients who were staying for three days or a week or more. There was a magical element to Kripalu. My defenses were down. Thoughts circled my head, things I hadn't taken out to examine for a long time. I was open to this experience.

I was in a group healing circle. We had been opening up to each other all morning. There was very little small talk. Knowing I would never see these strangers again gave me comfort. It was a new experience, women asking to look at truth, people who were hurting who wanted to heal. Someone in the group said it was okay to feel grief. Someone else gave me permission to not be perfect. I was asked, "Regan, why are you really here today? What is your intention for your work today?"

Instead of making up a cover story or a quick lie, I did something entirely uncomfortable and different. I told the truth.

In a small group of women, all very open, earthy, and accepting types, I was asked to state an intention for the session. We were supposed to talk about not only what was on our minds, but what was weighing heavily on our hearts. Big difference.

We were directed to talk about what we didn't want to talk about. I was told to share my secrets, my sadness, my pain. And in return, I was asked for nothing. Well, except to listen. We had to all be quiet and simply listen. No one was to offer advice or to interrupt. It was called a sacred sharing space, whatever that meant.

It was an exchange that I did not know. My only job was to be still and quiet and listen when another woman shared. And then it is was my turn. I was going to share with strangers. I was compelled to do the opposite of what I'd normally do.

The session flowed. Everyone seemed to be telling truths. One woman was dedicated to losing twenty pounds after struggling with overeating her whole life. She realized it had very little to do with the food and everything to do with her addiction. Another woman was intending to get out of an unhealthy relationship, to value herself, to leave a man who brought her little joy. I was slightly resentful toward her strength. She was doing something I couldn't do until I was forced to. But then the woman leading the group, or guiding rather, said something about how we made changes only when we were in enough pain. It seemed she was talking directly to me.

The women looked at me. It was my turn to share. I quietly inhaled and stated my intention—to make peace with my daughter's death. I said I wanted to let go of the guilt. To forgive myself. I told the truth about the accident. The end of my share came and I saw faces of compassion. The room was silent. No one was offering a solution or advice or even judgment. No one was telling me how to feel. I was accepted in that moment. I had stated the facts of what happened, I poured out my feelings, and I met with peace. It was a new experience for me. I was exactly where I needed to be. There may be judgment, but if it was there, the women were silent and I didn't hear it.

It was time to meditate now. I was thankful for the quiet. I needed this time to unplug.

Once I heard that praying was asking and meditating was listening. I was trying too hard to do both. Lately, I'd been pissed off at God, so I was no longer certain to whom I was asking.

Or to what or it or if anyone or thing was even listening.

I was angry. I was so angry at God. My mind raced in a fit of rage. I was angry Grace was mangled in such a way I barely recognized my own daughter. Metal stabbing through angelic, flawless skin. What God did that?

I needed to quiet my thoughts. I was supposed to be relaxing, letting go, thinking of nothing. All I could see was the concrete, the inside of the car, and hear the sounds of cars smashing and my daughter's voice. It was haunting.

But really, somewhere beneath it all, I knew I was angry at myself.

Later, in what was called "group work," which was basically glorified group therapy, I said it out loud.

"I'm so angry at God." It helped to share, as much as I hated doing it. "Where was God?" I asked to no one in particular. It was a statement more than a question.

I ached.

It was a wild feeling to be at the receiving end of a therapy session. In my social work, I was familiar with asking the questions and suggesting and guiding. There was some sense of freedom in asking for help, letting go and doing what I was told. I was willing and I had an open mind. This was new and I wondered from where it was coming. It hit me.

I'm not totally broken. I'm just really, really fragile.

Later, at the lunchtime meal, delicious organic and vegetarian, I was biting into a dark green leafy concoction drenched in freshly ground sesame seed dressing when a woman from the group came up to me and handed me a slip of paper. She didn't work at Kripalu, but she was a longer term guest of some sort. She had access to the reading material room and she jotted down a passage for me.

It was attributed to Jesus.

"When you make the two one, and when you make the inner as the outer and the outer as the inner and the above as the below...then shall you enter...I am the Light that is above them all, I am the All, the All came for the from Me and the All attained to Me. Cleave a piece of wood, I am there; lift up the stone and you will find Me there."

Chapter Twenty-seven

I softened.

I guess I was willing to hear the message because a feeling of appreciation swept over me, whereas a month or two ago, it would have been detachment. Reading a passage attributed to anything religious would have turned me off. I would have pushed her away, the woman who handed me the slip of paper. But today, I embraced the stranger. I said thank you. I even reached out and hugged her. Then I sat by myself, as we were instructed to do, and ate my meal in silence. I read the passage about a hundred times.

My thoughts spiraled. I breathed in deeply, feeling an ounce of gratitude. I acknowledged the feelings inside of not understanding. Not understand anything. What was there to understand?

Then, like a lightning bolt, I heard a voice. It was my own voice, inside my head, and it said, *"God's Grace."*

God's Grace?

Now, I could come up with two explanations for this. At the dinner table, we learn to say grace. I also knew the expression, *By the grace of God.* But the explanation that worked for me was God's Grace at work in my life. Grace was God's. She was God's Grace.

She was of this world. She came from my body. But she was of something more powerful than me.

At that moment, I handed her to God. I can't explain it and still don't understand it, and perhaps I never will.

But in that moment, right there sitting alone at the lunch table, I understood what I cannot explain. She was of God.

Then, something unexplainable began to happen. I slowly began to feel less alone than I had in months, and I grasped that she, my Grace, was not in pain.

She was God's Grace. And I made a pact to try to see God's Grace every day.

I wasn't there yet, but I felt the healing begin.

Then, the calm came.

Chapter Twenty-eight

Regan didn't hear the footsteps. It was the sound of a pop that jolted her.

She turned and red wine flowed into a goblet. The hands of a man gripped the stem. She moved her gaze up, followed the forearm, the dark skin still stained from summer, up to a strong shoulder, finally resting on a face that looked so familiar. Yes, she had seen him on TV and on book covers, but there was something else. He even felt familiar.

He caught her looking and his eyes met hers. She didn't move. He looked away. Walked away, with nothing more than a casual, "Evening" thrown her direction.

Perhaps she had imagined it. She surveyed her surroundings.

She had the perfect spot on the angled white couch. Right in the corner where she could see the book-lined shelves and the pretty decorative items displayed on side tables and on stacks of books. Most of the candles were lit. The circle sconces looked lovely set upon the square coffee table. Boggle and Checkers were among the staples. Regan inhaled the scent of musty old board games and books. She tucked her feet under her and sat Indian style. Nowadays, the preschool teachers called it crisscross applesauce. It annoyed her. But Grace sat that way and used the expression, so she came to love it. Her toes found warmth under her thighs. The fire crackled.

He reappeared and set a glass of red wine down by her seat. She smiled a thank you, took a sip, and went back to savoring the fire's glow.

Chapter Twenty-nine

She felt a jolt inside. His voice was so masculine and scratchy.

"How was your walk?" This was all he said.

He sounded so rugged. It was all that registered. Very unexpected.

Regan turned to face the handsome bearded man. She didn't like how uneasy she felt. It was like he was looking directly into her. She hated it. Wanted it to stop. She restrained herself from reaching out and touching his beard. "Do you always stare at people?"

"No, just the pretty ones." His response irritated her, but it was hard not to crack a smile.

Who was this guy? She sipped her wine, running her fingers through her hair.

"Obviously, the fame has gone to your head." She regretted saying this the instant it came out of her mouth. She didn't want him to know she knew who he was.

They were sparring now. She didn't have energy for this, but she kept at it. He remained silent.

"For your information, I'm not a fan. I only recognized you from the poster at the bookstore. Everyone in town seemed to be talking about your arrival." She tried to backtrack.

"Yes, well, I don't crave the spotlight as much as I used to," he admitted. Regan was caught off guard. She expected a monster-sized ego.

It was true, Regan thought to herself, that he had stepped out of the limelight. She remembered hearing press about it. Seemed people got more popular by disappearing. Less was more. Didn't Leonardo do that for a while? Or Johnny Depp? Julia Roberts? A low profile kept the interest.

But that wasn't why he did it. He walked away from the fame to concentrate on more authentic writing. She recalled a clip on *60 Minutes,* or one of those shows.

Okay, admit it, you know who he is. Her gears were churning overtime. The voice in her head was jogging on the gerbil wheel.

She looked up. She felt the warmth of the fire hot on her face. She felt him staring at her.

Awkward.

She quipped, "Don't you have some place to be? Like a bookstore or somewhere?" She was completely unsure of herself. The attitude of confidence she had with Jack and Leo vanished.

He hesitated for a moment, taking it all in, and then spoke. "Actually, the book signing got cancelled due to the snow. It's just as well. I'd rather stay here and hear your story."

She paused.

"What?"

"You don't even know me." She laughed, annoyed but slightly flattered.

"I'm curious. Who is this woman in such a rush she bangs into strangers, doesn't apologize, and lands in the snow? A weeping snow angel," he said, more like a statement than a question. He didn't let it go. "I want to find out, who is the weeping snow angel?" This was definitely a question, Regan noticed.

Regan remembered the figure in the window earlier today. Did he always say what he was thinking?

"We are the only two at the inn." He glanced over his shoulder to see who else was around. "Well, you, Gerta, and me. And I know she's an early bird and has already retired for the evening."

Retired? Who even says that? Does he really speak this way? What's your point? Regan was thankful she was filtering her thoughts before she spoke.

"Even the four-wheel vehicles are in for the night," he said.

He couldn't stop looking at her. She could barely look at him.

"You look a little too comfortable sitting here. Don't want you to fall asleep on me." Who did he think he was? "How about if we bundle up and walk down to the Heritage? Gerta said it stays open until one a.m. even in the storm. The Heritage Tavern, let's go. How about I challenge you to a few games of darts? Think of me as an old friend. I'm Samuel. Call me Sam. And I know your name, you're Regan. Hope you don't mind. I asked Gerta who the rude woman was staying at the inn."

Regan looked up. He was smiling, and she laughed, smiling too. The ice was broken. She brought her eyes to meet his and she forced a stare. *One, two, three, four, five.*

She held her gaze while counting under her breath. He made her shudder inside.

"Okay, old friend, you're on. But get ready cause you're going down." Regan was secretly good at darts. Her ability to hit the target was uncanny. She had ridiculous eye-hand coordination. "I'll bet you a round of Guinness I'll beat you," she baited him.

He said with a smile, "I prefer Black & Tan. Round's on me. I'm old school like that. Girls, excuse me, women, don't pay. I like to take care of my date."

"Oh really? Is that how you roll?" She laughed. "Well, suit yourself. You can pay. But this isn't a date. And I'll still win."

Samuel played along. Who was this woman? His stomach was doing somersaults. He was having fun. What a great feeling. It'd been far too long since someone caught his attention.

Chapter Thirty

If true love could happen in a night, then this was what happened.

In life, there was one lesson taught through the ages — savor expectancy, but have no expectations.

It could also be said, with one hundred percent certainty, people should expect the unexpected.

The stars aligned, the snow fell, and love descended. One had known the heartbreak of adultery, death, guilt, and loss, and the other knew the pain of loss, guilt, death, and helplessness. They were the same, these two; the earth smiled on them. It didn't take long before they gave in and smiled back.

Hours into the dark but magical night, Regan felt the red wine and espresso wear off and seep into her veins. She was exhilarated and exhausted. She wanted to pinch herself. After the sixth dart game — yes, she won, but it was unclear if Sam was a gentleman or if he simply was lousy at darts — the two strangers, who felt like old friends, stopped completely after about several beers and wines later.

Sam pulled his chair in closer. Where did the hours go? Regan inched in. She took in his scent. She could almost feel his rough beard against her soft cheek. Inhaling, he said the most intense words a man had ever spoken.

"You are intoxicating."

And then, he said something that captivated her.

"You feel like home."

Her defenses had fallen away hours earlier. The first time he placed his hand on the small of her back as he guided in through doors of the townie tavern, firmly holding the door for her, she felt protected. She felt safe with Sam.

He found an old mahogany booth. The locals stared. Many said hello. They knew him in these parts. Word had spread about his appearance. No one gawked, but no one was rude either.

She initially tried to push his hand away. This wasn't a date. She could open her own door. And then he put it back. And he pulled out the booth bench, and he waited until she sat, and he ordered for her after finding out what she liked. He took care of her more this night at the Heritage Tavern than Noah had done in their years of marriage.

And she let him.

The entire evening, Regan craved his touch. Different than Leo. Certainly different than the poet or Jennifer.

With Samuel, she was on fire. A deep, dull roar that was lit on her morning walk, which had no intention of extinguishing. The heat welled up. She could not stop herself. He saw her every move. No one had watched her like this. No longer alone in this world, he was there beside her. Looking in her eyes. Stroking her hair. The only transition from being total strangers to lovers was a matter of hours from the early morning light to the sparks by the fire to the quiet bustle of the local tavern.

There was little small talk. They learned what they needed to learn, but it didn't seem to matter. It would all be figured out. Tomorrow, or the next day, or in a month, or a year, or in ten years.

"Oh, I've loved her so long." Sam said this directly to her. She knew he was stealing lyrics from Neil Young. She didn't care.

He moved into her side of the booth. All the other booths were filled with couples or friends sitting opposite one another. They were back in junior high school, goofy and flirty and unable to keep their hands to themselves. For Regan, the feeling was giddy.

By the time they ordered their second appetizer, Regan stopped battling. He told her he had not felt this overwhelmed in years, and she believed him.

They made plans to spend the following day together. Then one more night at the inn. Then they went back to their own lives. She would begin hers. He would continue his. They would learn more about each other that would help them chart the course for the next few months.

They talked and talked into the night.

"Sshhh. Don't think. Just marry me." Yes, he said this. Yikes. Fuck.

"What?" Regan was at a loss for words.

"I know, it's insane. Hold the thought. What I mean to say is that one day, you will marry me. You will, if you want to. If we want it. We could do this." He didn't need an answer.

She laughed, but knew he was not joking. "I'm going to marry you."

"Question or statement?" Sam waited for her answer.

"Statement," she interrupted. He knew she was not kidding. "Just not tonight."

"Okay, deal," he joked. "Let's save something for a rainy day."

Samuel Kellogg. Sam Kellogg. Sam.

She liked the way his name rolled off her tongue. She listened to and devoured this man who had walked into her life with no warning. She wanted him to stay.

He was at least a decade older, probably fifty or so, and he had never been married. She was surprised to learn he had no children, no ex-wives, very little attachment.

He had been close to marriage several times, but they ended the same way, almost always. They'd want marriage and he'd want out. It wasn't too hard to let go of these women. Beauty was around every corner for a successful, somewhat well-known and attractive man. He played it safe, almost always selecting a woman whom he knew he didn't love. They needed him more than he needed them. Not the marrying kind. Not the girls you took home to Mom.

Regan discovered through their marathon conversation that his parents died when he was young. It was a sad story, and Regan could tell he had told it many times. He didn't express much emotion with the details about the fire until Regan grew silent and locked in on him. She didn't take her eyes off his eyes except for watching his lips move, pronouncing words like fire, death, burned, loss, and guilt. She wondered how a little boy could go through life carrying that much pain.

Lana, the most recent lady in Sam's life, was beautiful, glamorous, fun, and also a whole lot of crazy. She had been diagnosed with Borderline Personality Disorder and didn't like the dull feeling she got when she took her medication. It took the edge off of her adventurous spirit—think Angelina Jolie from *Girl Interrupted*. Lana lived in her own version of reality. For a while, Sam accepted it—her fun times and her ups were almost addictive. But her demons inevitably reared their ugly heads and drama and chaos began to fill her pores. And then seep out, making a stable relationship nearly impossible.

Sam worked hard to forget his past. Living with manic women gave him a high. All the different women kept him from being restless, kept him from feeling the loss of his parents and his brother at ten years old. He was guilt-ridden over starting the fire. An accident, he still felt as though the matches were a murder weapon.

After becoming a man of faith—after doing the therapy he put off for too many years—he began to realize he would never fix himself by fixing others. When Lana tried to kill herself, he knew he could not make her any better, and by staying with her, he was making his life worse. He didn't want crazy anymore.

Sam grew up in Greenwich, Connecticut and summered in the Berkshires. It was the life his family had before the fire. And a close family friend took Sam in after the fire and raised him to be independent and fierce. Real men didn't cry. Pull up your boot straps. Go out in the world and make something of yourself.

This wealthy friend of his father who took him in paid for boarding school, took care of his trust fund until he was 18, and off to the best colleges he went. He never looked back, except for now, finally stopping after all these years. He purchased an old farmhouse that reminded him of the home he'd spent summers in up until the fateful fire.

His most recent book and motivation seminar series was titled □ □□in□ □□□□ It became an instant bestseller. People identified with the never-ending search.

Sam had this uncanny ability to relate to any person, regardless of history or income. He suspected it was time to begin to live authentically. He had to practice what he preached.

Regan connected with this thought — she had to leave what she didn't want, or what she no longer had, behind before she could figure out how to begin. She loved this man. Down deep, she felt their souls connect. As cliché, cheesy as that sounded, it was true.

Sam and Regan decided to spend their day in Stockbridge. He would show her his life there. He listened as she talked about Grace. He opened up to her about losing his parents and his brother. Through the night and into the next day, and maybe for forever, they would heal. The potential was there. It was a bold plan created in the late hours of a romantic snowy night.

"Goodnight, Regan. It was my pleasure. I can promise you this. I will not sleep tonight."

They held each other outside of her bedroom door. He was a gentleman. Kissing her softly, parting her lips slightly, but resisting his desire to open her mouth with his tongue. He felt himself growing firmer and thicker as he embraced Regan, but he stepped back and knew not to rush. There would be time. Even a lifetime.

She shook her head. "This is unbelievable. How could this happen?"

He interrupted her with a, "Sssshhhhh," pressing his finger to her lips. He took her head and embraced her, touching foreheads and exhaling deeply. "Goodnight, beautiful. I'll wake you at ten. We'll skip breakfast and have an early lunch in town. I'll show you around. Sleep in a bit. I'll bring you coffee—just cream, right?—when I come to wake you."

"Okay," was all she could say.

Before bed, she leaned against the door. Her mind raced.

It was as if they met long ago on a summer vacation to the beach, he was her summer love, and she never forgot him. And then he found her again. He came to her and, this time, he would not let go. And the timing would be right. She had the freedom now to choose the life she wanted.

Then, as unnatural as it felt, she knelt down, unfolded her arms, and placed them in prayer position upward toward her heart.

"God," she said, "I don't know what the hell, oh, sorry, what on earth is going on, but you've gotta have something to do with this. I'm going with it, if that's okay with you. I have to believe that you and Grace are watching out for me. Please, God, please, Grace, don't let me get into something I can't handle. It feels like I'm naked and exposed and can't swim. I'm drowning. But I feel like this is what you want for me. I'll be watching for signs. Oh, and thank you. I haven't said thank you for anything lately. So, uh, yeah, thanks, God. Really."

She got off her knees, climbed up, dropped her clothes, and fell into the sheets.

No counting sheep. No counting to one hundred. It became the most peaceful sleep she had in weeks. She could smell him on the ends of her hair, on her wrists.

And she smelled Grace too. She was sure of it.

She was near.

Chapter Thirty-one

She dressed deliberately casually but sexy. She wanted to look like this all the time, as if it were effortless to look this good. Naturally applied makeup. He'd think she wore hardly any at all. Her leggings were cute and tight, paired with the sassiest boots she had packed. □□ *ne* □□□ □□□□□she thought. But it was the only word to describe them.

Everything cried out, *t*□*u*□□ □*e*□*e*□□*r*□□*e* □*e*. And he did. Many times. A shawl hung past her hips and just over her bottom, a fitted turtleneck because it was winter, but it unzipped in the front giving way to a small dose of cleavage if she wanted to expose it. She didn't. Not yet. Then a delicate, hand-knitted long and thin scarf, draping its way down her body. He would later pull her close to him using it, loosely wrapping it around her neck and untangling her hair with his rugged hands. She would melt with his touch. They would share cappuccino and fire and wine and dreams. They talked effortlessly about sharing a lifetime.

He'd notice her layered socks, sassy boots, and trendy fingerless gloves. He'd observe how the silver, oversized man's watch clunked loosely around her delicate wrist. He imagined how beautiful she'd look in his rust-colored sheets, her skin tone the perfect shade of earthiness. Simple diamond studs would look elegant in her ears. Her lips were glossed in a cross between bronze and rose and blush.

Underneath, he would discover a nude bodysuit. Her breasts were full and nipples erect for him. Her scent would fill him. He'd think of being inside her, filling her. He would imagine and accept never making love with another woman. He would make her his.

Sam showed Regan the new wood floors he installed in the old farmhouse he was renovating. He used trees, had the wood planed down from huge oaks from the property his parents once lived on. The doors to all of the bathrooms were also from the Berkshires. It seemed more like a rustic cabin than a country farmhouse.

"I can't believe you know how to do this," she said.

The details impressed her. Small things like the light plates in slate, the battered concrete counters, the cork floor in the kitchen, and, of course, the wooden planks from the trees from his family estate. The original window panes had been refurbished and stained glass windows were hanging perfectly from the ceilings in rough pewter chains.

Everything about this man spoke to her. She noticed all of the elements of wood, fire, stone, and nature. Rock and water and a wall fountain. She heard the sounds of running water and was certain she smelled lavender in the air. She tasted faint musk or bark on her tongue.

He was so masculine, but paid attention to the kind of details that would matter to her. His book collection went on for six rooms, not pretentious, but well-cared for. Built-ins, candles, subtle ladders lining the walls.

Life in Samuel's home was orderly but lived in. He didn't alphabetize his collections, thank God, but he did take the care to have sections. She could tell how his mind worked, he studied in chunks, in topics. She liked everything about this man. Then she caught herself imagining her belongings in his home, if it ever was their home. Would there be room? She pushed the thought aside and remembered that she moved on tomorrow. He must have read her mind, because he asked if she could imagine herself between the walls. "Can you see yourself at home here with me?"

She didn't answer. The moment passed.

The day went on and disappeared into the night. Time stood still. It also rushed past her. She felt no judgment from her new lover when she shared about Grace's death and the texting.

She felt heard, accepted.

He saw her.

He loved her.

He wanted them to be together.

Now.

Chapter Thirty-two

He made love to her into the night, her body moving with his, sometimes slowly, sometimes in a more intense rhythm, hers wrapped in his, protected, eyes wide open.

They agreed to leave an opening for a life together, but time was a first step. It was a risk walking away, but they agreed to trust the process. God brought them this far, perhaps they would find their way back.

It was Regan's decision to step away. She needed to be on her own for a while, to be independent and understand what life without Grace was like. At this moment, life without a man did not compare to life without Grace.

Before checking out of the inn, Regan played the last day and night over and over in her head.

She was beginning to find Grace again.

The end

Beth Jannery is the Director of the Journalism Program where she teaches writing and communication for George Mason University as a full-time professor outside of Washington, DC. Beth started her journalism career at 21 for CNN's Investigative Reporting Unit. She has been a journalist, worked at Harvard University's John F. Kennedy School of Government and taught communication for American University in Washington, DC and Marist College in New York. She lives in Northern Virginia where she writes and raises her daughters, Skye and Tess. Beth earned her master's degree in journalism from Boston University.

Fiction
"Finding Grace Again"
"The Admiral's Daughter" (California Times Publishing, 2014)
Unapologetic (current project)
Non-fiction:
"Shut the Hell Up! 101 Reasons to Appreciate Your Life" (Rainbow Books, 1998)
"Simple Grace – Living a Meaningful Life" (Publish America, 2007)
"Simple Grace – Daily Joys" (Blurb, 2008)
"Simple Grace – A Journal for Your Journey" (Blurb, 2008)
"Simple Grace – Awareness, Meditations, Breathing Space" (Blurb, 2009)

Made in the USA
Middletown, DE
09 December 2014